weavers

Other books by Kate Avery Ellison

The Curse Girl

Once Upon a Beanstalk

Frost (The Frost Chronicles #1)

Thorns (The Frost Chronicles #2)

weavers

KATE AVERY ELLISON

For Jennie

WEAVERS: THE FROST CHRONICLES #3

Every day, life in the Frost grows increasingly perilous for its inhabitants. The Farther occupation continues, and food is becoming scarce. Lia Weaver's family is facing increasing perils, too—Jonn pushes his health to the brink as he works to uncover the mysteries of Echlos, and Ivy risks everything to get food for the family. And for the second time, the Weaver family is harboring a fugitive, but Lia doesn't trust her.

Lia has personally braved many struggles—a Farther occupation, family secrets, a heart torn between two men, and Watcher attacks—as she struggles to keep her family safe. But now, she will face her greatest challenge and uncover the Frost's deepest secrets as she completes her most dangerous mission yet for the Thorns.

ONE

THE WORLD WAS as cold as death's breath and just as dark as I eased open the front door of my family's farmhouse and slipped outside. Blackness that was tinged with blue wrapped around me like a cloak, and the chill of the Frost rushed into my lungs as I took a breath. The ache of the cold went to my bones as I walked alone into the forest, carrying a lantern.

I walked a little way into the darkness until I reached a clearing framed by the suggestion of trees at the edge of the shadows, and I stopped. My heart pounded and my shoulders itched from the unshakable sensation that unseen eyes watched me. I set the lantern in the snow, and it cast little slivers of light in a circle. The wind blew, ruffling my hair and stinging my cheeks. I waited.

Crunch.

Every muscle in my body drew tight as a bowstring. I held my breath.

Crunch, crunch.

Footsteps.

The tension in me eased as Adam Brewer slipped from the shadows. The black shirt and pants he wore helped him blend with the darkness as he stepped into the clearing, and his pale blue cloak was the same color as mine—the same color as the snow blossoms that would provide us with tenuous protection from the monsters that lurked in the night.

Seeing him made me feel both safe and nervous in some inexplicable way. Danger clung to him like smoke, but at the same time, being in his presence made me feel secure. We were friends, compatriots...and we might have been something else. But we weren't. We couldn't.

Adam's eyes met mine. His were dark, framed with black lashes—pretty eyes in an otherwise lean and sharp face. He was always watching, always restlessly thinking and organizing details in his brain. It gave him a wild look, but I knew now that was a misjudgment. He was careful, clever. His expression challenged me in the way it always did, unvoiced yet still apparent. He didn't say much with his words, but every glance and gesture he made hinted at something more, something quiet and intelligent and wonderful. I wondered again as I always did how I'd missed that aspect of him before. Or perhaps he'd kept it hidden on purpose, hoping we'd all think him a stupid oaf incapable of cunning and secrets, because Adam was one of the smartest individuals I knew.

"You're late," I said, just to say something.

He smiled at me—a quick flick of his lips that vanished almost as soon as it appeared. He was like that, always chasing his smiles with frowns. "I didn't think you were going to come. I know you've had your hands full lately caring for the latest fugitive you've taken in..."

"I said I would, didn't I?" I said it quickly, because right now I didn't want to think about that mess.

"Lia Weaver," he murmured under his breath. "Keeper of oaths." Faint amusement sparkled in those dark eyes.

I liked the way he said my name, *Weaver*, without condescension. To most people in the village, the word *Weaver* was an unglamorous moniker, a label that means only long hours, manual labor, ragged fingers, and tired eyes. It did not inspire admiration like Elder or Mayor or even Baker. Adam spoke the word like it meant something—like it was another word for strength, courage, or wit.

He glanced past me at the house, perhaps checking the windows to see if they were all dark. "We have only one more hour before sunrise. We'll have to move quickly."

I nodded. When had anyone ventured into the forests of the Frost and not moved quickly, with every glance over his shoulder straining for the sight of Watchers? Our trip would be no different.

"Ready?" he asked.

Fear churned in my stomach, but I didn't dwell on it. I drew my shoulders straight and lifted my chin level with the distant line of black forest that marked the Frost. With one hand, I reached up to touch the snow blossoms hanging around my neck. It was a nervous habit with me. I just wanted to be sure they were there. "I'm ready."

We plunged into the depths of the Frost together. The trees curled around us like fangs in the mouth of some ancient monster, and the bare branches snagged at my cloak and hair. I ducked down, my boots whispering across the hard shell of frozen snow, my eyes on Adam's back as he moved ahead of me. Here, everything was dark, but my eyes were adjusting and I was beginning to make out the path ahead.

We walked quickly and said little, although our silence was a conversation in itself. He paused to hold back a branch for me. I moved to his side as I heard a rustle in the bushes, and his hand brushed mine as he signaled for me to pause.

Awareness prickled over my skin. Suddenly, everything went deadly silent except for the pounding of our hearts and the ragged rasp of our breathing in tandem. We scanned the darkness, but nothing stirred against the pale line of snow. We exhaled in unison, exchanged a glance, and moved on.

The blackness was almost luminous as the faint light of predawn began to paint the snow silver beneath our feet and along the edges of the tree limbs that touched the sky. I rubbed my arms for warmth, although I was more than cold. Seeing the Frost at night conjured up flashbacks to a time several months ago when Adam and I had trekked through the night to find the Thorns' secret gate, accompanied by Adam's brother and Gabe, a

Farther fugitive who'd fled from the southern country with the help of Thorns operatives.

Gabe. Just thinking about him made my stomach twist into painful knots.

Adam held up a hand, jerking me back to reality. I heard the sound of branches snapping.

My terrified exhale escaped from my lips in a ghostly spiral, white and clouded in the freezing air. I mouthed Adam's name. Holding a finger to his lips, he grabbed my wrist and pointed.

The darkness formed a solid curtain, so it was impossible to see what was moving through the forest ahead of us, but the faintest gleam of red light sparkled off a line of icicles hanging from one of the rocks. My heart turned to stone and dropped to my knees as the icicles shattered.

A Watcher.

Adam grabbed my arm and shoved me in the direction of the farmhouse. Out of the corner of my eye I saw the rush of blackness, the glint of glowing red, the shiver of light across a back of metallic spines. I ran. Adam was beside me, his hair streaming in the wind.

"Hurry," he shouted, but the wind snatched the word away.

The ground shuddered as the Watcher bore down on us. I clenched my teeth against the burning pain in my lungs and pumped my legs harder. Behind me I heard branches ripping. A snarl shuddered through the air. The branches dragged at my clothes and slapped me in the face. A sob caught in my throat. We weren't going to make it.

I felt a faint swish of wind as something sliced the air beside my ear. I swallowed a scream and tried to run faster, but I was slowing.

"Cut right," Adam yelled, panting.

We rounded a thicket of trees and suddenly he was shouting "here!" and I was slipping, stumbling after him under the low-hanging limbs and through the snowdrifts. We fell together into the shadows beneath the tree.

The Watcher thrashed in the forest a few feet beyond us as we lay on the ground, flattened in the snow and lying still as stones. I was spread-eagle, my cloak stretched over me and my body sunk into the freezing wet. I trembled as the monster searched the underbrush.

Splinters of red light skittered across the ice and danced on Adam's face. He was very still. His breath streamed up from his mouth in a wisp of white.

The Watcher snarled, and the guttural sound rattled me to my bones. I squeezed my eyes shut as he drew closer. Claws scraped rocks as the creature's hot breath filled the air with steam. Something fell beside my hand with a plunk, but I was afraid to look.

And then, with a hiss of wind and a scrape of tree branches, the Watcher was gone.

We stayed motionless, listening. I counted my breaths and listened to the wind. Finally, Adam let out a shaky breath and sat up, his sharp eyes scanning the shadows.

"I think it's gone. We're safe now."

I opened my eyes and looked around. Light stained the horizon, and the forest had shifted from black to a dull gray. I could see Adam's face clearly now—his jaw flexed as he gazed at the churned snow where the Watcher had been. He turned to me, his gaze flicking over me gently as he checked my visible limbs for wounds. "Are you all right?"

"I'm fine."

He nodded. He wasn't going to coddle me—I knew that. I shut my eyes again, gathering my strength. When I opened them, Adam was offering me his hand.

"Come on," he said.

I willed myself to take his hand and stand, even though my legs were still trembling and my whole body felt like wrung-out yarn.

We continued on through the Frost. There was no sign of the monster now, but unease hummed a song in my blood, and my movements were jerky, skittish. Adam's gaze flicked over the ground, and he took a few more steps before crouching and brushing his fingers over a patch of frozen dirt, clearing away small stones and pine needles.

"Here," he said, producing a set of blunt digging tools from his belt.

I joined him, and together we hacked at the crust of ice and earth. My back prickled with unease as I turned it toward the trees, but Adam was a bastion of calm. His dark hair brushed the tops of his eyebrows and hid his expression, but I could see that his shoulders were relaxed. My stomach gnawed with worry as I hacked at the dirt and wished for a shovel.

When the hole had grown sufficiently deep, Adam produced the items he'd been carrying beneath his cloak: a knitted net covered in snow blossoms that Ivy and I had worked on for weeks, a few extra cloaks, and a tin of dried meat. It was an emergency package for someone traveling through the Frost at night, someone seeking the gate or shelter from Watchers. He wrapped it all in oilcloth and lowered the bundle into the hole, and we scooped the dirt back over the place and patted it down before kicking the snow back into place. Adam made a mark—a long curved line with a shorter one branching off the side, like a misshapen Y—in the bark of the tree.

The mark of the Thorns.

Only a few weeks had passed since we'd completed our last mission. Now, we'd been burying such packs for weeks in an effort to prepare for the renewal of the Thorns duties my parents had performed when they had been alive, duties that had gotten them killed.

"How will someone see that in the darkness?" I whispered, running my fingers over the mark.

"It's not just the tree," he said. "You'll learn to memorize the landscape as well." He turned and gestured at the trees around us. "See how they clump together in thickets here? There's a stream over there past the rocks and a clearing beyond it. And that rock looks almost like a man. See the neck, the head?"

I studied the place where he pointed, trying to commit the details to my memory. These night excursions were part of my training. Adam had begun to train me more thoroughly as a Thorns agent, teaching me what I'd need to know to survive in the forest or conduct spy work in the village. My life could depend on these lessons.

We continued on, slipping through the trees that were just amorphous shapes in the near-darkness. The snow crunched beneath my boots, and I could smell earth and pine and the cool wet scent of ice. We broke through the forest into a clearing. A field. Across the huddled, snow-covered stalks of grass, I saw the black waters of the river, and beyond it, the road.

The Farther road.

It was too dark to make out the wagon tracks that crisscrossed the frozen dirt like scars on a mangled cheek, but I knew they were there because the sight of them was branded in my memory forever. Soldiers carted prisoners along this road all year long. From one such wagon, Gabe had escaped across the river and into the Frost. The wind blew against my cheeks, teasing water from my eyes.

Adam's hand brushed my shoulder—a single, light touch. A question. Was I ready? The moonlight glinted off his eyes. In response to his unspoken words, I stepped forward into the field toward the road. I was ready.

We reached the river. Here, the sky loomed over us, steel gray and too big, and I shivered. I couldn't feel safe under such a large sky after a life beneath the trees. The water glittered like ink as it glided past, smooth and unstoppable. Once this river had formed the boundary between the Frost and Aeralis, the place the Farthers would not cross. But no longer. Now, they had spilled over into our land, bringing with them their oiled weapons, their crude mechanical technology, their glove-clad cruelty.

Adam crouched beside the water and dug another small hole. He filled it with supplies and marked the place by drawing the Thorns symbol on the trunk of a sapling above it.

I stared across the river at the road as he worked. The sense of danger I felt looking at it mingled with a sudden, intense need to stand in the place where so many others had made their escape. I turned and scanned the bank of the river.

There—a fallen tree stretched across a shallow point like a bridge. I jogged down the bank and scrambled up the roots. My heart galloped. My mouth was dry. I grasped the rough bark of the tree and hauled myself up.

Adam followed at my back like a shadow. I expected him to grab my arm, hiss in my ear to stop, to tell me to wait for him while he crossed alone. But he didn't.

The tree trembled as I crossed it, but it bore my weight easily. I reached the other side and jumped down. The Frost was at my back. Aeralis's border was before me. A shiver spread over my skin. I tingled from my scalp to my fingertips. I'd never been on this side of the river.

Adam landed beside me. I caught the flash of his quick smile in the blackness.

"I just wanted—" I began.

His voice was just a tickle in my ear. "You've never been across the river, have you?"

The warmth of his breath against my skin made me flush. I nodded and moved away an inch. There was tension between us now, a dance of avoided topics and guarded looks. Perhaps the unlikely attraction had always been there, lurking just beneath the surface. But since I'd almost kissed him in the barn a few weeks ago, the feelings had grown into a thrumming heat that filled every word, every look, every interaction. I didn't know how to deal with it. He'd become woven into the fabric of my existence, mingled with the air I breathed. If I reached out, he was there. If I spoke, he answered.

Still, we were separated by a gulf of unspoken feeling that neither of us would express.

Adam noticed when I pulled away slightly, of course, because he noticed everything. He didn't comment, and his face kept the same neutral expression. But his shoulders stiffened, and when he spoke again, his voice was carefully controlled.

"We should bury the last one by the road."

He'd been the one to rebuff my advances, but still I caught him staring at me sometimes, his gaze wounded before he hid it behind his careful mask of studied indifference.

Perhaps he was right. I had cared deeply for Gabe, but I'd thought I'd never see him again, so I'd been prepared to relinquish any hope of that love. But now...now there was a chance that I would, and Adam seemed convinced that I would want to rekindle the romance I'd barely had time to explore. So we danced on, our lives in tension and harmony simultaneously as we skirted our feelings and masked our hurt. We'd become a team, working in tandem. We had no time for this attraction and so we didn't address it. But I still felt the heat simmering in my blood, and judging from the way he was holding himself slightly apart from me now, so did he.

We climbed the bank to the road, and I breathed deeply. Faint light from the horizon glanced off ridges of frozen dirt. Snow lay in the deep places where the wheels had ground into the earth, frothy and white like puss in an infected wound. The road lacerated the land and marred the beauty of the landscape. It was a Farther invention through and through, as ugly as a gun and just as chilling to look upon.

Adam touched my elbow to get my attention. He pointed across the road toward Aeralis. "Do you see it?" A light glimmered in the far darkness as it shot across the sky like a fallen star. I nodded.

"Airship," he said simply.

I watched as the light traced an arc across the sky and vanished. Wonder and fear swirled in me. What must it be like to fly through the night like that?

We dug the final hole beside the road, on the shoulder where the prisoners might stop to stretch their legs as the soldiers smoked. I pressed a line of stones into the packed clay, forming the symbol that would be so easily overlooked if one didn't know what to see.

When we'd finished, we stood and stared together down the road.

"I've never been this far south," I said. "This is the first time I've crossed the river."

Adam watched me, not saying anything, just letting me talk.

I wanted to say more—I wanted to verbalize the feelings swelling inside me, the anxiety and frustration and longing—but I couldn't frame them into words. They slipped away from me, dissolving into unnamable emotions whenever I tried to speak them. So instead, I watched the sun begin to rise against the horizon, where the Aeralian fields stretched into a smudge of black that would eventually become Astralux if we walked far enough. The wind whipped my hair and teased the edges of my cloak. I felt so empty, so fragile, like a glass just waiting to be filled.

"We should get back," Adam said finally. "We've done enough for one trip."

We climbed back down the bank and crept across the tree stretched over the river. Adam assisted me as I scrambled down to the bank, and his fingers were just as cold as mine. I noticed he winced as he handed me down. Then, I saw the dark stain on his sleeve.

"You're bleeding."

He glanced at the place and shrugged. "Just a scratch."

I remembered the sound whooshing past my head when we were running. The monster had mauled him? A fresh shudder ran over my skin. "Adam..."

"I'll be fine," he said. He wiggled his fingers to demonstrate the functionality of the arm and gave me a tense smile. "It's just a scratch," he repeated.

Only when we'd stepped back into the shadows of forest did I breath easily again. It was ironic that I felt safe now, here in the Frost, but... Some things were less frightening only because they were familiar.

Picking up our feet, we hurried toward the farm.

TWO

WE RETRACED OUR steps through the snow, hurrying because of the growing light. Despite the dangers, there were Huntsmen and Trappers who would venture into the outskirts of the Frost by daylight, and we could not let them find us here. Our presence would cause questions, suspicions. Perhaps even accusations. The reward for captured Thorns agents was great.

Slowly, the world around us turned white with sunrise. When we reached the edge of my family's farmyard, I took the last few steps alone. I turned once and looked over my shoulder at Adam. He leaned against a tree, not looking at me, probing his wound with his long fingers. His forehead was knit with mild concern, but he hid it when he realized I was watching.

"Are you going to come in?" I asked. "I can clean that."

He straightened, adjusting his sleeve again. He frowned as if he was weighing the pros and cons of agreeing, and finally he nodded.

My twin brother, Jonn, looked up from the kitchen table as Adam and I entered the house. Papers and charts were piled on the table around him, and bags lined his eyes. He blanched as he saw the blood on Adam's sleeve, but his voice was calm and cool as if we were discussing the cow. "Watchers?"

I nodded. No need to elaborate—the single word sufficed. It told the whole story in one succinct bite.

Jonn frowned and leaned back over his work as I fetched a bottle of medicinal whiskey and some clean rags to use for bandages from the pantry. Adam leaned against the wall with a sigh and pulled back his sleeve to better see the cut while he waited. "Progress?" he asked Jonn quietly, indicating the papers with a flick of his eyebrows.

I took note of their exchange quietly. Adam and Jonn had experienced some conflict in the past, but they were getting along better now that they were working together on Thorns business, a fact I had observed with pleasure and relief.

"Some," my brother said, dragging his fingers through his hair and rolling his eyes in exasperation. "I've figured out how to ignite the power source, but not much else." He indicated a diagram spread before him, where a sketch of scribbled ink depicted the mysterious device Adam and I had discovered a few weeks earlier. The PLD, or Portable Locomotion Device. It had originally come from Echlos, the ruined remnant of the Ancient Ones' laboratory hidden deep in the Frost and guarded by the Watchers. Our father's family had hidden it away and passed down the secret for generations.

I had many, many questions—we still didn't know why the Weavers had been entrusted with such a task

24

yet, for instance. It was just one part of an ever-expanding puzzle, one that perhaps went all the way back to the Ancient Days. But we were slowly working through my father's journals, unearthing the tidbits about our past that gave clues to why our family was linked to Echlos and this device. Jonn in particular had taken to deciphering the bewildering PLD documents as easily as if he'd been doing it his whole life.

I found the supplies to tend to Adam's arm, but I hesitated a moment in the doorway. My chest ached with sudden pride as I watched my brother conversing with Adam Brewer as an equal. His cheeks were flushed with exhaustion, and his eyes were glassy from pouring over documents by firelight, but he held his head high and his shoulders back with confidence. For most of his life, Jonn had been relegated to the corner or his bed. His twisted leg and bouts of headaches and seizures—the price of a childhood injury—disqualified him from being a fully functioning member of the Iceliss community. In our village, Jonn was viewed with either pity or scorn. But now, working with the Thorns, he pulled his own weight and received the respect that his contribution demanded. And he'd blossomed because of it.

"Does your father mention anything about the PLD in his journals?" Adam asked Jonn as I drew him to a chair and uncorked the whiskey bottle. I splashed some of the drink onto a rag and rolled back his sleeve. It was a clean cut—almost as clean as a knife. The blood had already begun to clot in a dark red line.

Jonn frowned thoughtfully as he considered the question. "Yes—but only bits and pieces, and in such a way that I almost always miss the reference the first time. Everything is coded or cleverly disguised. I think he worried his journals might fall into the wrong hands, so he hid everything important. I'm sure I'm missing something else—a vital piece that will bring it all together."

Adam shut his eyes as I dabbed whiskey on his cut. He shuddered but didn't make a sound.

"Maybe we should check the rest of the blankets," I joked, because the information about the secret location of the PLD had been cleverly hidden in my mother's Frost quilt, a "woven secret that kept us warm," as my father had always told us. We'd never realized the full extent of those words until we'd found the map stitched in the quilt. The secret location Adam and I had been searching for had been hidden right beneath my nose the entire time.

Who knew what else my parents had hidden away in this house, among our things?

Jonn snorted and shook his head in a way that told me he'd already examined them all. He leaned back over the papers and scowled at them.

"Where's Everiss?" I asked, glancing around. Like the predictable gentleman that he was, Jonn had insisted that she take my parents' old bed, the one he used to sleep in, while he slept by the fire. Usually, she was awake and up by daybreak, anxious to pull her weight around the house.

The tips of my brother's ears flushed pink as they always did at mention of the newest fugitive to take refuge in our house. "She's still sleeping. She was up late helping me with the journals."

"What?" I slammed the whiskey bottle down so hard it sloshed. "What are you thinking? Helping you with Thorns business? She's a *Blackcoat*. We can't trust her!"

His eyes blazed. "She brought us the PLD. I don't see why she can't know more about it. And even if she still had Blackcoat sympathies—and she doesn't—who's she going to tell? She's stuck here with us. Everyone else thinks she's dead."

I looked to Adam for help.

He met my eyes, but I couldn't read his thoughts in his expression. "He has a point—she *is* injured, sequestered, and totally at our mercy."

"For now," I said. "But what about when she's fully recovered? What if she runs off and tells the Blackcoats everything?"

"She's not going to do that," Jonn snapped. "She came to us. She brought the device to us. She could have given the PLD to them—to the Blackcoats—but she didn't. She brought it here."

I wasn't convinced. We'd simply been Everiss's best bet for survival—nothing more. It wasn't loyalty or goodwill that had led her to the farm. It was pure, unadulterated self-interest. "I don't trust her."

A small cough came from the doorway of my parents' bedroom. We all turned.

Everiss smoothed a hand over her sleep-rumpled curls and bit her lip. The rims of her eyes were red, but she gave us a smile as if she'd heard nothing. And perhaps she hadn't. "I was just going to start breakfast...but I seem to have interrupted a discussion. I'll just work on my weaving until you're ready for me to join you—"

"We're done talking," Jonn said firmly, shooting me a look that could have singed the hair off a horse. "Please stay."

I clamped my mouth shut and turned away. I would continue this discussion with him later.

Everiss ducked into the bedroom again and reappeared with a basket of yarn. Her gaze drifted over Adam and his injured arm. Her eyebrows lifted, but she didn't ask any questions. She knew better than that. Taking one look at my face, she moved to Jonn's side, where she slid into a chair and bent over the basket.

We no longer considered each other friends, I supposed. She knew I was furious about my sister's involvement with the dangerous and revolutionary group of young people in the village who called themselves Blackcoats—an involvement Everiss had not prevented or warned me about, even though Ivy was only fourteen. And so we avoided each other. She stayed glued to Jonn's side, and I spent most of my time with Adam, trekking through the Frost.

There seemed to be a lot of places I tried to stay away from lately, I mused darkly. I was avoiding the village, too, because in the last few weeks, things had begun to take an ugly turn there.

Adam touched my arm lightly. I flinched, and he withdrew his hand instantly. "We should speak outside," he said in a low voice. "We have something else to discuss."

I nodded.

"Privately," he added, when I looked reluctantly at Everiss and Jonn. I didn't want to leave them, because now they would discuss what we'd been talking about. I just knew it.

I followed him out, and we walked in silence to the barn. As soon as the door thudded shut behind us and the warm dark enfolded us with the sounds of the animals, I whirled.

"I cannot believe he's telling her things about the PLD. She cannot be trusted. Is he blind?"

"Lia," Adam said.

I choked on an incredulous laugh. "It's ridiculous. Of course he is—he's being blinded by his feelings for her. The day she came to us for shelter, he told me he loved her. And for all we know, she's using that to her advantage. His affections are making him a fool."

"It happens to the best of us," Adam said softly, almost bitterly.

That shut me up. I took a step back and leaned against the door, studying his face. We stared at each other, and I saw pain pass like a fog over his eyes. The emotion evaporated as quickly as it had come, and once again he was focused and intent.

"You're right to be cautious," he said. "But give her a chance. I've spoken to your brother at length about this. Jonn believes she'll want to defect and work for us."

"For the Thorns?" I didn't know what astonished me more—the news about Everiss's possible change in loyalty, or the fact that apparently Adam and my brother were having long, voluntary conversations together now. "And you support this idea?"

He nodded, thoughtful. "Another agent would help us tremendously. Her duties would be limited, of course—the whole village thinks she's dead, so she can't show her face there again." He raised an eyebrow at me. "That's another reason for her not to betray you. She has nowhere else to go. The Blackcoats all live and operate in Iceliss."

"As far as we know," I muttered.

He made a fair point, though. Of course, he assumed Everiss would behave rationally—I did not. Many people did anything but the rational thing when it came to what they were passionate about.

"Let it rest, at least for the moment," he said. "Right now she's helping your family with quota and healing from her injures. Any talk of her staying or leaving is still weeks away. There is time."

"You're right." I leaned back against the door and tried to massage some of the tension from my temples with suddenly trembling fingers. "It's just..."

"You've been betrayed and deceived before," he finished. He took a step closer to me, reaching for my hands to tug them away from my face. "I know. You have every reason to be suspicious now."

I laughed under my breath. Betrayed. Deceived. How true. Everyone in the Frost seemed to have a secret. My parents had been secretly smuggling fugitives through the Frost to safety before their deaths, unbeknownst to everyone, even Jonn, Ivy, and me. Cole Carver, the village buffoon and my fervent admirer, had turned out to be their murderer. Adam Brewer, the silent lurker and near-outcast—whose family everyone had blamed for my parents' deaths—had turned out to be the Thorns operative working alongside my parents. The cruel Farther noble who'd recently taken up residence in the village was Gabe's brother. And even my best friend, Ann was a secret Thorns operative. I'd only discovered it a few weeks ago.

So many secrets.

Was it any wonder that I felt wary?

I let him pull my hands away, and suddenly we were face to face, with his fingers warm against my wrists and his eyes searching mine. I turned my head; he let me go.

My pulse hammered hot under my skin. I cleared my throat. "You said we had something else we needed to discuss?"

"Yes," he said, stepping back to give me space, letting me breathe again. "The PLD. We're running out of time."

"Jonn is making progress," I said.

"Yes, but we might not have that much time. We need something else. We need a leg up on this decoding process."

"And how do you propose that we do that?" I asked.

Adam studied me thoughtfully. "Korr has information and research on Echlos. He was looking for the PLD. Recently, he was asking questions about your family in the village, particularly about your father. He mentioned journals. Perhaps he has documents, information that might help Jonn with the decoding. Another journal, perhaps. The missing piece."

Another journal? I inhaled sharply.

"You really think so?"

"It's a long shot...but from what I know of Korr, I don't think he would have come here in the first place if he didn't have confidence that he could make the device work. I've heard rumors lately that he has a document that originated from the Frost." Adam hesitated. "He must still have it, even though he regards the PLD as lost. And I need you to try to get it from him."

My heart stuttered at the thought of getting anywhere near Korr again, but I swallowed and nodded.

"I'll do whatever you need me to do."

THREE

MY FOOTSTEPS ECHOED as I took the path through the forest toward Iceliss. A bag of extra yarn dangled from my hand, yarn I could use to trade for more food. Bluewings fluttered overhead in a cacophony of thrashing feathers. Ice dripped from the trees and made puddles on the ground. The snow blossoms that lined the path dipped and waved in the wind, a blue frenzy of scent that seemed more fragrant today. Spring was still just a faint memory lingering on the edge of the wind, but it was coming. We called it The Thaw.

We had weak springs and short, brutish summers. The air was never truly hot in the Frost, but every year for a few months the snow melted and the grass grew tall and the chill retreated into the nighttime hours. We had time enough to grow a few meager vegetables and harvest enough dried grass to fill our barns, and then the winter overwhelmed us again. We had no autumn season. Winter began with the first of the storms that brought ice and snow down upon us.

My heart sank like a stone when I reached the Cages that led into the village proper, but my steps didn't falter. I strode between the Farther soldiers guarding the entrance to the steel-enclosed tunnel that was supposed to protect us from the monsters as if I didn't fear them. As always, a chill slipped down my skin as the shadows cast by the metal beams flickered over my face and arms. On the other side, the snow blossoms still danced in the wind, and the tree branches scraped and rattled against the bars. The sensation of being a rat in a trap closed around my throat, threatening to strangle me, but I forced myself to walk slowly, almost languidly.

Finally, I reached the gate to the town. Steel met old stone where the Cages emptied into the village. Houses and shops of snow-weathered rock, faded from eons of ice and sunlight, huddled together around narrow streets. Smoke from a few cooking fires curled toward the sky in spirals, and somewhere I heard the sound of children chanting in unison as I passed the school, the newest addition to our village.

The new school was Farther-taught. Raine had brought a teacher from Aeralis, and this severe Farther with the sharp eyes and a sharper tongue drilled the children daily in their lessons. None of the village families wanted to send their children...but for those who attended, their families received extra food and supplies each week. And so the classes were filled to the bursting, because our people were hungry. The winter had been long, and the occupation had been harsh. We were feeding soldiers and the workers who built the Cages and Farther houses of steel and brick. We didn't have enough for everyone, not anymore.

I slipped past the new schoolhouse on my way to the market. They'd built it next to the quota yard, and the children used the space in the yard weekly to drill in "movements" that looked suspiciously like military exercises.

Farther soldiers marched through the streets in a stream of gray uniforms and glittering buttons, heading my direction. I froze. My eyes slid past them to the wall, and my stomach simmered with uneasiness. I felt like an insect waiting to be crushed every time I entered the village now. I carried so many secrets—the Thorns, Gabe, and now Everiss, too.

What if they knew? What if they were coming for me?

The soldiers passed without stopping, and I exhaled deeply. Ducking my head to hide my expression of relief, I turned the corner of the quota yard and headed for the market.

The collection of shabby little shops and stalls seemed even more meager today. Few people had anything extra to barter. I browsed the selection of fish and sized up the cured squirrel meat one Hunter had brought. It was more gristle and bone than meat, but we needed nourishment, and I couldn't be too picky. I held up what I'd brought to barter—yarn—but the man shook his head.

"I need salt, Weaver. I can't feed my family or preserve what I hunt with your wares, as prettily woven as they are."

I lowered my eyes. Slowly, I put the yarn back in the bag. "I understand."

His mouth turned down, and he nodded at someone behind me. "Maybe she'll take your yarn." With a sniff, he moved away and began speaking to a Baker trading day-old loaves. I turned and caught sight of a familiar red cloak and hood. The Mayor's daughter. My best friend.

"Ann!"

She hugged me so tight that my hood slipped from my hair. She felt bony in my arms, like a bundle of sticks wrapped in cloth.

"Lia. How are you?"

Her eyes searched mine. She didn't ask about Everiss, of course, but I saw the questions on her face. Everiss had been more Ann's friend than mine before she'd changed into someone we didn't know. It was just one more painful change in a long list of things that had become so different over the last few weeks and months.

"Hungry," I said with a harsh laugh, gazing down at the yarn in my hands that the Hunter had just rejected. "Like everyone else."

Ann followed my gaze. "Oh, yarn," she exclaimed with a little too much enthusiasm. "What luck—I need more yarn for the mittens I'm making. I'll trade you some food for it."

I wasn't fooled for a moment. "Ann..."

"No," she said, insistent. "I need that yarn, truly I do. Come on."

I followed her up the hill to the Mayor's house, my heart sinking with every step. I could read the story in the sharp thrust of her shoulders through the fabric of her dress, in the sunken curve of her cheeks, in the fragility of her wrists and neck.

She was hungry, too, but she was pretending.

We reached the house and passed through the garden to the back entrance, the kitchen. The cook was gone, and we were alone. Ann went to the pantry and opened the door. She angled her body to block it, but not before I saw how bare the shelves were.

"I have some bread," she said over her shoulder. "It's a few days old and a little crusty, but still filling."

"I...that's fine," I said. My chest felt heavy.

"Excellent." She wrapped it in oil paper and presented it to me. "An even trade."

I bit my lip and let her tug the yarn from my hand.

"How are...things?" I asked.

She held up a finger. While I watched, she went to the door that connected the hallway between the dining hall and the kitchen. She placed her ear against it for a moment, listened, and then stepped back with a nod of her head. It was safe to speak freely.

"Things are, well, the same," she said with a grimace. "Officer Raine has taken up residence in this house now, you know. His men repaired the damage to my father's study, and he has refurbished it to his own taste. He no longer makes any pretense about his power over us."

"And Korr?" My heart did a nervous dance just saying his name. Gabe's brother was a cunning, dangerous man who asked too many questions. He'd seen me at the lake the day Everiss was shot, the day Luka the blacksmith died. He knew I'd been looking for the PLD, but as far as he knew, it had gone into the river and been lost. And he'd protected me—he'd told the soldiers to let me go, and then he told me it was because he knew I'd helped Gabe escape. He didn't know I was with the Thorns.

I didn't know what he thought about me. Did he believe I was with the Blackcoats? He hadn't called for my arrest. He hadn't said anything to Raine.

Yet.

I wasn't about to relax when it came to Korr. He'd let me go, but I didn't trust him for a second. He was dangerous, unpredictable, and clever. He had power over me because of what he'd done, and those who held power like that always took advantage of it sooner or later. I knew one day he'd use that power to get something from me, something he wanted. The question was only what...and when.

"Korr has taken up residence here," Ann said. "To keep an eye on Raine, he says—and to torment him, I think. They do not get along. They snarl at each other like dogs both wanting the same bone."

"I'm surprised Raine hasn't hung him from the trees yet."

Her lips tugged apart in a rueful smile. "Officer Raine is afraid of him, I think. They have a history."

The bread was heavy as a stone in my hands. I saw Ann look at it a few times, but she dragged her gaze away. I ached to give it back to her, but my stomach knotted, and I thought of everyone at home. We were all hungry. We all needed food.

And there wasn't enough.

I dragged my mind away from that. I had other things to worry about, too. My new assignment from Adam. The PLD. We were running out of time.

"Ann," I said. "If Korr had something he wanted to keep safe, where do you think he would keep it?"

She frowned. "You should probably stay far away from Korr."

I couldn't do that. "Where, Ann?"

She bit her lip. "He has his office in the new Farther building...you've been there."

An uncomfortable silence wrapped its tendrils around us. I'd been interrogated by Korr after Ann had given him my name—something I'd only later learned was due to her being an agent and under orders. It had not been the brightest moment in our friendship.

"All right," I said. "But is there anywhere else where you think he might keep something important?"

"In his room here, perhaps," she said. She shifted uncomfortably and averted her eyes. "But I really don't—"

"Show me?"

Reluctantly, she motioned for me to follow her. I put the bread down and together we went through the kitchen door and into the hall. Sunlight glanced off polished wooden floors and glittered on lamps and chandeliers. It seemed even more opulent than I remembered.

"Raine had things brought in from Aeralis," Ann explained in a whisper.

We crept up the staircase to the second floor and went left, into the guest wing. Ann stopped at the third door and touched the knob with her finger. "This is his room," she mouthed, and then she gestured for me to head back downstairs.

I hesitated. I put my hand on the knob. Surely it would be locked...

"Lia," Ann hissed, and I dropped my hand and followed her.

But a plan was already brewing in my head.

~

I checked the traps on the way home. One gaunt, half-starved squirrel. It was pitifully inadequate to feed four people, but we'd have to make do. I trudged for the farm, mulling over the things I'd seen and heard in the village.

Jonn worked at the table while the meat cooked. He had pages of notes spread around him, and stacks of my father's journals formed a wall at the far side of the table. He scribbled and sketched and occasionally stopped to turn the PLD from side to side, staring at it with a scowl of concentration before bending over the journal in front of him once more.

"Making any progress?" I asked, joining him at the table.

He didn't look up from the page he was scribbling words onto. "Some."

So he was still angry with me. I suppressed a sigh. "Jonn..."

"I'm working, Lia."

I left the table and went to check on the meat. I was boiling it into a stew. At least that way it might stretch a little further.

Everiss watched me as I stirred the pot. Her eyes reflected the fire, and she held her injured shoulder stiffly as she worked. It would probably always bother her now, just like Jonn's leg always pained him.

Maybe they had more in common than I thought.

I chased that thought away quickly. The idea of Everiss and my brother was utterly nonsensical. And how could we continue to hide and feed her for the rest of our lives? It was not a sustainable plan, not in the long run.

The stew wasn't finished cooking. I sat back on my heels and looked around. I didn't see Ivy anywhere. Jonn was still working steadily. Everiss sat quietly, yarn in her lap. She didn't look at me.

"I need to talk to you," I said, stealing a glance over my shoulder at Jonn's back.

He didn't raise his head to look at us. He hadn't heard.

Everiss's fingers went still in a way that suggested she'd been expecting this. She set the yarn aside and clasped her hands together in her lap. "Yes?"

"In private. Perhaps in the bedroom?"

She followed me. I shut the door and leaned against it. She sank onto the bed, her face carefully neutral and her mouth pressed in a determined line.

A shiver of apprehension ran through me. At the moment, I would rather run through the Frost without snow blossoms than have this conversation.

"Adam tells me you are interested in joining the Thorns," I began.

She rubbed her injured arm and avoided my gaze. "Yes, if they'll have me."

"Why?"

Her eyebrows drew together, and she lifted her chin with a defiant jerk. "Well, everyone else thinks I'm dead. I have nowhere to go. And in case you forgot, the Farthers destroyed my father's life and scattered my family. I have reason to want them all gone."

"We help *Farther* fugitives," I said. "And you Blackcoats hate all Farthers. Don't you think it's a conflict of interest?"

"Our greatest interest was justice," she said. "It always was."

"That's utter nonsense."

Her eyes blazed. "You don't know anything about it. You refused to join."

"I refused to join because it was utter nonsense."

"Jonn says—"

"That's another thing we need to discuss," I interrupted. "My brother."

Everiss winced. Clearly, I'd hit a sore spot. She knew she was leading him on. I felt equal parts vindication and dismay. Poor, lovesick Jonn. She was going to break him.

"It's not like that," she said, clasping and unclasping her hands. "I care about him. We wrote letters for years. He's—he's my friend."

I wasn't backing down. "Does he know that your feelings tend toward friendship only?"

She bit her lip and didn't reply, but guilt shone in her eyes.

I scowled. Well, I wasn't surprised. Jonn was about as subtle in love as a yelping puppy. But still...frustration rose in me like a wave, threatening to spill from my mouth in the form of angry words. Ignorance of his feelings might have induced me to forgive her. Now, my dislike was even stronger. She knew, and she did nothing to stop it. At best, she was being careless. At worst, malicious or manipulative.

"You're going to break his heart, Everiss."

"I've been meaning to speak with him," she mumbled, fidgeting with the edge of her dress and avoiding my eyes. "There hasn't been a good time. I don't know what to say."

Suddenly, I felt bone-weary. She wanted me to give her an answer, a plan. A command, even. "I'm not your Ma," I said, standing to my feet and crossing my arms. "I'm not going to tell you what to do. But know this—if you hurt my brother, you'll answer to me."

I left her sitting on the bed and returned to the fire to check the stew. It was bubbling and hot. I went to fetch the wooden bowls from the kitchen.

Jonn lifted his head from his papers as I crossed the main room for the kitchen. His eyebrows pinched together. "You and Everiss are talking again?"

"It wasn't a friendly chat," I said, instantly annoyed at the hope springing into his eyes. Was he imagining some storybook happy ending where Everiss and I became best friends again, and then she fell into his arms with protestations of love? He was sharp-witted, my brother. Surely he knew how silly such a fantasy was?

But on the heels of my anger came sadness. With his seizures and withered leg, he'd had a hard life. Was it so foolish of him to want a little happiness, as unlikely as that might be?

I was angry, but not at him. I was angry at the way things were. The Frost, the snow, the hunger, the never-ending work making quota and fearing Farthers and hanging out our blossoms to protect us from the monsters in the night. We were like fish holding our places in a fierce-flowing stream, ever swimming against the current but never going anywhere. I blinked and saw my life in a flash before me, unspooling like so much thread, cycles of frost and thaw and work and weariness that culminated in a misplaced snow blossom or a misguided word to a Farther soldier. Blood on the snow. A quick, brutal ending to a quick, brutal life.

For a moment, I couldn't speak.

44

"Lia?" Jonn said, reaching for his crutch.

I shook off the paralyzing melancholy and turned for the kitchen. "Where is Ivy? It's time to eat." I practically growled the words.

The door banged open before I even finished my sentence. My sister was on the stoop, slinging off her snow-covered cloak and stamping her feet to warm them as she stripped off her mittens.

"Ivy," I snapped. "Where have you been?"

She held out her mitten-clad hands. "Gathering winterberries. I thought we could eat them fresh for dessert."

Berries would stretch this pathetic meal a little farther. "Fine," I said. "Put them in a bowl and grab the bread."

She hurried to comply. "Is there any milk?"

Milk. That reminded me. "Have you seen to the animals this evening?"

Her mouth opened and closed. I took that as a no. "I'll do it," she said quickly.

That was the moment Everiss chose to emerge from the bedroom. I crossed to the door. "No, I'll go. You bring the scraps for the chickens."

She nodded and looked down at the berries in her hands. My gaze slid past her to Jonn and Everiss, and I saw them lock eyes. His ears warmed. She looked away.

Frowning, I went out into the snow.

The barn door squeaked as I shoved it open. I took a few steps inside, humming tunelessly under my breath. As I reached for the grain bucket, a sound like a shoe against stone scraped in the near-darkness by the horses' stalls.

"Ivy?"

But something about the thick silence that followed made the hairs on the back of my neck rise. I pushed myself up and fumbled for the snow shovel leaning beside the door. I raised it in the air like a weapon. "Who's there?"

The shadows shifted, and my blood froze in my veins.

A figure stepped out from behind a support beam, and my fingers curled around the handle of the shovel. A man. He was thin and bundled in a thick gray coat. His close-cropped, steel-gray hair gleamed against his olive skin.

A Farther?

Another glance confirmed it was true, but he wasn't in uniform like the soldiers roaming the village.

A fugitive?

I didn't have the luxury of puzzling over his origins at the moment. I was still very much alone with him in the barn.

"Don't move," I said. One glance confirmed that he was too close and I was too far for me to make a run for it without being intercepted. No, I needed to convince him that I wasn't afraid. I lifted the shovel.

His mouth turned up at the gesture. Clearly, he didn't find me remotely threatening.

"I mean it," I said, my voice cracking sharply and my arms beginning to burn from the weight of the shovel. "I'll hurt you—"

"I am looking for Aaron or Eloisa Weaver."

My parents? Suddenly my lungs were empty of air.

"Lower your weapon," he murmured, reaching into his coat.

46

I tensed, expecting a gun. But what he withdrew shocked me. A broach in the shape of a Y. It glittered coldly as he held it out for me to see.

"I am with the Thorns," he said.

FOUR

THE MAN LEANED against the opposite wall and tucked
the brooch back into his pocket as I stood rooted to the
ground, struggling for words. Slowly, I lowered the
shovel and sagged back against the wall. Was this a trap?
Did I dare admit to knowing what he was talking about?
He could be anyone.

"Thorns?" I asked.

He made an impatient noise in the back of his
throat. "You know," he said, confident as his gaze
searched my face. "Don't waste my time, girl."

"Where did you come from?"

He was not from the village. He was Aeralian, but he
wasn't one of the soldiers—I'd never seen him before in
my life.

A fugitive? He didn't look like any of the thin,
frightened, starving escapees that found their way
through the forest previously.

The stranger grimaced, a quick twist of his mouth
that hinted at volumes of unspoken memories. "I've
journeyed here from southern Aeralis," he said.

He pulled a pipe from his pocket and stuck it
between his teeth. From his other pocket he produced a
match, lit it with a swipe against his shoe, and cupped
one hand around the pipe as he touched the flickering
flame to the tobacco inside. A tendril of smoke curled up,
and I frowned. He pretended not to see. He tossed the
match onto the flagstones by my feet, but my eyes didn't

stray from his to look at it. I stepped on it with my heel, grinding the ashes into the dirt. He half-smiled around the pipe, as if he'd been interested in my reaction to his lighting up in our barn.

"I crossed the border into the Frost this morning, avoiding your village and keeping to the forest to stay clear of the soldiers," he said.

The soldiers. My stomach danced nervously at the realization that once again, I had a Farther in my barn. Was this one a fugitive like Gabe had been? "What do you want with my family? Are you seeking shelter?"

He inhaled smoke and gave me a short, spare smile. "No. I am sorry to intrude like this, but I must speak with your parents, and I dare not wait until nightfall to make my presence known. Where are they?"

A moment of small shock followed the question. The air felt like ice against my skin, and my heart thumped loudly in my ears. He asked so casually, so expectantly— as if they were right around the corner, right outside. It made the pain of their absence that much keener as I answered him.

"My parents are dead." The words fell out of my mouth like stones, clattering in the silence that immediately followed.

His eyebrows lifted in shock, and his eyes drained of expression. They were flint-like as they stared into mine, daring me to admit I was lying. "Dead?"

"More than six months ago," I whispered.

"I am sorry. I didn't realize..." His voice trailed off, and he took another puff of the pipe and scrutinized me again, really looking this time. I could see him taking in my age, my slight frame, the bags under my eyes, and my bony wrists. I probably looked like a child to him. "Who has been completing the missions?"

49

The man was waiting for me to speak. I took a deep breath. "Me."

"You?"

I lifted my chin, feeling defiant. "Yes, *me*."

I waited for him to express more disbelief. But instead he blew smoke out of his nose like a dragon and gestured at me with the pipe. "What is your name?"

I hesitated. Was this another test? "What is yours?"

He smiled again, but it was less spare than the last time. "I am called Atticus by my friends. We don't keep many names in the Thorns. It makes us harder to trace." He paused, waiting for me to reciprocate.

"Lia Weaver," I said grudgingly.

"Lia. I am impressed—not only by your determination to defend yourself using that shovel, but by the fact that you've taken on your parents' responsibilities here."

"I—"

"I am sorry to be abrupt, but if your parents are gone, then there is another person here who I must see," he interrupted. "It is very urgent. I believe he goes by the name Brewer now..."

"Adam," I said. *Of course.*

Atticus paused. "You know him? Can you contact him for me?"

I was already racing ahead in my thoughts. How much should I say, how much should I conceal? Could I trust this man?

"Yes," I answered. "But it's complicated."

"Complicated?" Atticus's tone sharpened. "How so, girl?"

"The Farthers—your Aeralian soldiers, I mean— guard the village day and night. They've erected caged walkways to keep out the Frost monsters, and they carry guns. It is difficult to contact anyone without arousing

50

suspicions...and I have no reason to go back to the village today. It will be dark soon..."

I could always put out the lantern to signal him, but I wanted to test this man first, discover the extent of his resolve.

"And your 'Watchers' come out at night, yes?"

"You've heard of them?"

He laughed, and the mirthless sound wheezed from his throat like a cough. "My dear, I am a Thorns operative. I know things. Besides, who hasn't heard of the mysterious creatures that roam your forests? In Aeralis, they tell whispered tales of the beasts with the glowing red eyes and the long, sharp claws. Little children safe in their Aeralian beds have nightmares about your Watchers."

Gabe never told me this. No wonder the Farther soldiers had put up the Cages around the paths. But I didn't have time to ponder this glimpse into the Farther mindset, not now. I crossed my arms across my chest and looked Atticus in the eye. "Then you know how dangerous the Frost can be. And yet you are here."

He tapped the ashes of his pipe against the flagstones. "My business is my own." He lifted his head and looked past me at the slivers of light coming through the cracks around the barn door. His eyes, I noticed, were deep silver. They were odd-colored eyes for a Farther. "It grows late," he said, impatient now. "How far to Adam Brewer's house?"

I tugged open the barn door. The wind blasted against my cheeks, and I winced. Already the sun had begun to slip toward the horizon. The fading sunlight seeped across the snow like melted butter, turning everything golden and strange. I tasted the wind and smelled the sharp scent of pine, the ever-present reminder of the forest that surrounded us. "Miles," I said.

"Do you know the way?"

I stepped back, facing him again. He seemed determined to see Adam, determined enough to brave the dangers. I would put out the lantern, then—

Footsteps crunched in the snow outside. Atticus flattened himself against the wall, his silver eyes darting to mine. I saw the question in them—was it soldiers? I shook my head in an indication that he should stay silent.

A voice rang out. "Lia?"

Ivy.

Taking a deep breath, I relaxed my eyebrows and mouth into a blank expression and stepped outside. I pulled the door shut behind me and leaned against it. Splinters dug into my back. My fingers tingled with sparks of nervous fear. "Ivy," I said.

She held a bucket of scraps in both arms, slop for the chickens. Her gaze shot to my face, and her expression turned suspicious.

"Lia, where have you been?" Despite her defiance, fear simmered beneath the edge of her tone.

"Just finishing up the chores," I said, my words crisp, precise. "I'll feed the chickens, too. Is the table set for dinner?"

"No," she said. "I was helping Jonn put away his papers. He needed to lie down. He was getting the tremors."

My heart squeezed with worry. Jonn's seizures were violent and unpredictable. They came and went without warning, and often they were preceded by drowsiness. I wanted to run straight in to check on him, but there was a Farther in my barn, and I had to take care of that first.

"Go back to the house. Tell...tell *her* to put out the plates and the food." I didn't want to speak Everiss's name in front of this man, in case he was some sort of spy. The impulse was silly, though, because he already knew who and what I was. If he worked for Korr, then I was already as good as dead.

I reached out and tugged the bucket from her hands. She let go of it, and the rim bumped against my shin through the fabric of my skirt as the bucket swung between us. She turned around, and I held in a sigh as I watched her head back to the house.

As soon as my sister disappeared through the door, I turned around and returned to the barn. Atticus was waiting, one shoulder pressed against the wall. He'd put away his pipe, and he faced me with his hands in his pockets. "Little sister?"

"Never mind her," I said firmly. "I want to keep my family out of this."

He lifted an eyebrow at my tone, but didn't comment further.

I set down the bucket and brushed the hair from my eyes. "You can stay here in the barn tonight. I'll put out a signal—if we're lucky, he'll see it and stop. If not...I'll figure something out."

"And the monsters?"

I pulled off the snow blossoms that hung from my neck and tossed them at his feet. "Keep quiet and wear these. You'll be fine. There are horse blankets in the back, and you can bed down in the hay. I'll bring you something to eat later."

"Thank you."

A wry smile twisted my lips, followed by a surge of pain. This all felt so familiar, and yet so different. Another day, another Farther in my barn.

Atticus observed my sudden sadness, and I could tell he was making mental note of it. His scrutiny reminded me of Adam, and it was unnerving. Turning my head to hide my expression, I retrieved the bucket of scraps and carried it to the chicken pen.

"I'll be back later," I said. "Stay quiet. If anyone comes, hide."

My gaze strayed to the false door in the floor, then snapped away before he saw me looking. I wasn't ready to trust this man with my parents' secrets. Not yet.

~

I hung out the lantern just as night began to fall, and the flickering light from the candle spilled bits of shivery gold across the snow. I stared a moment at the wall of gathering black that was the Frost as I thought about the stranger in our barn, with his cool smile and watchful eyes.

After a moment, I turned back for the house.

The evening progressed quietly. Everiss and Ivy worked on quota by the fire. I took stock of the grain and other foodstuffs we had left for the week. Jonn poured over our da's journals. He scrubbed both hands through his hair and sighed in quiet frustration as he worked. Everiss kept stealing glances at him, but she didn't speak.

I paced to the windows to gaze at the lantern glowing in the dark. Every time I checked it, my heart skipped a beat as I thought of the beasts that prowled the night. But no Watchers stirred in the darkness. The hours ticked by, and finally sleep tugged too hard at my eyelids to be ignored, so I tumbled into bed and fell into a fitful sleep. Ivy's soft snoring punctuated the silence along with the moaning of the wind, and I tossed and turned as I drifted in and out of dreams of Thorns symbols, brooches, and glowing Watcher eyes. Finally, when dawn began to stain the edges of the window curtains, I rose and put on my dress. I couldn't sleep any longer. I needed to check on the fugitive, ask him more questions. I didn't know why Adam hadn't come, but I'd have to handle this alone for now. I pulled on my cloak and stepped outside. The lantern had burned out.

I promptly ran into Adam.

"You came," I breathed. "Did you see the lantern? I waited almost all night."

"I was on a mission," he said. "I didn't see it—I was just checking in on you. What do you need?"

He studied me with his dark eyes, waiting for me to explain. I took a deep breath. "There's a man," I said. "In the barn."

"Another fugitive?" He looked across the yard. The wind stirred the ends of his hair and made them dance. His brow furrowed.

"Not exactly. He had a brooch. He said...he said he was a Thorns operative."

Adam swung around to regard me with surprise. "Did he give a name?"

"Atticus."

Adam blinked. The planes of his face hardened. "Stay here," he ordered, and then he turned and strode for the barn without another word.

"Adam!"

He didn't turn to acknowledge me, so I ran after him. The yard was white and white and white, and then grayness enveloped me, and I was passing through the yawning black of the barn's open door and into the soft quiet of the barn. I heard Atticus stirring in the hay.

Adam put out a hand, stopping me.

"Lia...?" Atticus called quietly.

"No. Me." Adam stepped forward.

Silence filled the room. I caught my breath. The shadows didn't move. Behind us, the early morning light shone through the crack in the door, painting a streak of blue-white light across the floor.

"What are you doing, Atticus?" Adam spoke softly, angrily.

A match flared to life, and Atticus's face was framed in flickering gold. Shadows carved a scowl on his mouth. "Adam. It's about time you showed up."

"What game are you playing?"

The match went out, plunging us into darkness again. I tugged open the door, but Adam's hand stopped me. He didn't want our voices to carry. Nodding, I fumbled for a lantern.

"Game?" Atticus laughed, low and disbelieving.

I found the lantern and lit it with a match from my pocket. Light filled the room. Atticus had risen to his feet, and he and Adam were facing each other. Adam stood taller, his shoulders taut and his head thrown back as he faced the other man. Atticus's gaze cut to me and slid away.

Adam crossed his arms over his chest and tipped his head to the side. His voice dropped to a growl. "What are you doing here, Atticus?"

"Things are bad in Astralux. I had to get out before I was captured. Rumors are floating around...rumors of a leak among the operatives. The Aeralian dictator is getting desperate. He's tightened security, increased the raids. The Trio—"

The Trio?

Adam held up a hand to interrupt him. "Lia," he said without turning to look at me. "You should get back to the house."

"I think she should stay," Atticus said.

I paused, one hand on the bar. My heart beat fast.

"And I think she should go," Adam responded. "And I'm the leader here."

I turned back to them. They faced each other, tension written into every line of their bodies. There was more at stake here than the surface issue of me, I could sense it.

"Ah," Atticus said. He lifted a finger. "That's where you are wrong."

Adam stopped. He raised both eyebrows in annoyance. "Oh?"

"The Trio has appointed me in charge of the Frost operation."

"What?"

"I'm relieving you of your position." Atticus spoke the words with the delicate air of a man placing a knife against another man's throat.

Adam stilled. He blinked twice, the only thing that betrayed his utter shock. His expression stayed smooth as he repeated, "You're relieving me of my position."

"Yes. I was given the orders yesterday. You're not in charge here anymore." Atticus reached into his pocket and produced the pipe. Unscrewing the handle with deft movements of his fingers, he pulled it apart and produced a rolled up slip of paper from a hollow space in the handle.

Adam snatched the paper from his hand and unfurled it. His forehead furrowed as he read the missive. He didn't speak. He glanced at me, but less because he wanted my reaction and more because I was just a place to put his gaze, I think. He looked at the floor.

"We can talk about all this later," Atticus said. "Right now I need to get to a more secure location. Adam?"

"Sir," Adam said. His tone was clipped, respectful, frosty.

Atticus turned to me. "You will receive more orders soon. Until then, you're doing good work here, Lia Weaver."

"Thank you," I said.

As I watched, they both exited the barn and vanished into the forest.

FIVE

I FOUND ADAM'S note pinned to the barn door as I was heading inside to feed the cows.

Meet me at the Brewer farm this afternoon for training.

The paper shivered in the wind like a tiny white bird. I crushed the note between my fingers and stared at the woods, thoughtful.

After I'd finished tending the animals, I pulled my hood up over my hair and went back to the house for my snow blossoms.

"I'm going out for a bit," I told Jonn.

Everiss looked up from the yarn in her lap, but she didn't speak.

"Where's Ivy?" I asked.

"She's in the forest," Jonn said. "Looking for winterberries."

I paused and looked pointedly at Everiss. "She's been in the forest a lot lately, hasn't she?"

Her cheeks flushed. "I haven't the faintest idea where your sister is, Lia Weaver. Don't act as though I do."

"You knew where she was a few weeks ago when she was running around with the Blackcoats."

Her eyes narrowed. "You're forgetting that I'm no longer a Blackcoat."

"And my sister? Is she still sneaking around like you taught her to do?"

"I don't know anything about your sister, Lia."

"I wish I could believe you—"

"Lia!" Jonn snapped. "Leave it alone."

He'd pushed himself halfway up, one arm braced on the table and one arm gripping the back of his chair. His face had turned red with the effort, and his eyes blazed.

I went out, slamming the door behind me. The wind fanned my face and cooled my cheeks, and I exhaled shakily. My brother was on her side now instead of mine, despite the fact that she was toying with his emotions, despite the fact that we couldn't trust her, despite the fact that we'd been best friends since birth. He'd chosen her over me against all reason and sense, and it rankled me deeply.

I headed into the forest and straight for the Brewers' farm.

~

The Brewers lived at the edge of the river that separated the Frost from Aeralis and beyond. I struggled through the snowdrifts alongside the black water, my lungs burning from exertion and my hands tingling from the cold. Finally, I spotted the low roofs of the Brewer farm. I surged toward them in relief.

A long, low-built log house backed up against a wooded hill. A barn and several paddocks formed two arms that enclosed an open space set up with wooden targets and a dummy stuffed with straw. At my approach, the front door of the house opened and a figure stepped outside.

"Lia Weaver?" It was Abel, Adam's brother.

"I'm looking for Adam," I said, stepping past the targets and around the dummy. "Is he here?"

"He's in the barn." His eyes followed me as I crossed the yard to the barn door. The hinges creaked, and a puff of warm air that smelled like oiled leather and dirt rushed over me. I saw someone hanging from a beam in a flood of sunlight that poured from a window set high in the wall.

"Adam?"

He dropped to the ground and faced me. He was wearing a black shirt and trousers. Exertion had tousled his hair, and a fine sheen of sweat covered his brow. His eyes swept over me, and the expression in them was impossible to read.

"You found my note, I see," he said finally, reaching for a cloth to wipe his face.

I nodded and stepped into the light, letting the door shut behind me. Most of the straw had been cleared away to reveal a polished wooden floor. Beams and ladders lined the walls, and thick knotted ropes dangled from the ceiling. It was Adam's training ground. I did not come here often.

I almost didn't catch the bundle of cloth he tossed at my head.

"Get dressed," he said. "We have work to do."

I pulled on the clothing in one of the empty barn stalls. Wearing boy's trousers always felt strange, but in a wonderful way. I had a freedom of movement that I'd never experienced before I'd begun training with Adam. Why women didn't wear trousers all the time, I didn't know. They were marvelous.

Adam made me climb the ropes and balance on the beams until sweat poured down my back and bathed my face in a sheen of sweat. "What is the purpose of this?" I demanded more than once, growling with effort as I tried for the third time to climb a thick, knotted rope to touch the ceiling of the barn. I could only ascend halfway up the length of rope before I was too exhausted to continue.

"Physical strength. Dexterity. The ability to run, climb, escape if necessary."

"From Watchers?" I let go and dropped to the floor with a grunt.

"From anything," he said, and pointed to the next obstacle. A long, flat board stretched between two ladders. I climbed onto it gingerly and peered over the side. The ground was very far away. My stomach turned.

"Does Atticus know about my training?" I asked between breaths as I tried to cross the beam without falling. I glanced at Adam and almost fell, but I caught myself.

He frowned at the mention of Atticus, but when he spoke, his voice was smooth and devoid of any inflection that might betray his emotions. "Atticus only knows what concerns him as leader, and this is not a matter of his concern."

I had my doubts about that, but I kept quiet about them. And why didn't he want Atticus to know I was training? Did I dare broach the topic of their previous acquaintance? "You and Atticus...you knew each other before, in Aeralis?"

"Yes." Adam's response was clipped. He grabbed my hands and helped me down from the beam, then released me abruptly and stepped back. I felt the distance between us keenly. He turned away, and I stared at his back.

"You don't seem to be friends."

"We were compatriots." He handed me a cloth to wipe my face without looking at me.

That wasn't really an answer. I bit my lip as he gestured for me to climb the rope again. My arms were shaking from exhaustion, but I hoisted myself up anyway. The muscles in my shoulders and back screamed in protest. "In the barn...he seemed to be alluding to something..."

"That's enough," Adam said, and I didn't know if he meant the exercise or the conversation. I let go of the rope and dropped to the floor, panting.

"No more for today," he said. "I don't want you to overdo it."

I bent over to catch my breath, and he moved past me and began fiddling with the equipment. When I spoke again, my voice came out low and quiet.

"Do you trust him?"

Adam froze.

I straightened, watching him. He didn't speak at first. His hands were still against the ropes. "Of course I trust him. He is a member of the Thorns. He's dedicated his life to the organization, and I've seen proof of that again and again."

"Do you want to do what he says?" I pressed, remembering the way Adam had acted in my barn, all still and formal when Atticus had assumed control.

Adam turned to face me. He lifted one eyebrow. "He is my superior. I don't have a choice. And neither do you."

I didn't find that answer satisfactory, but it was clear that the conversation was finished.

~

Jonn, Ivy, Everiss, and I finished the last of the bread and leftover squirrel stew that night for dinner. We all ate slowly, chewing carefully, savoring each bite, and sucking the juice from our fingers.

The table was quiet. Jonn wouldn't look at me, and neither would Everiss. They were avoiding each other's eyes, too. Ivy stared at her plate and wouldn't speak to anyone. The only sound in the house was the clink of utensils against the dishes and crackle of the fire on the hearth. The wind rattled the shutters and made the walls creak, and faintly in the distance I heard the low moan of a Watcher.

Ivy tensed at it.

We all held our breath and listened, but the sound faded and did not come again. I relaxed slightly. I looked at my brother until he lifted his head, and our eyes met.

He frowned but didn't look away this time.

We needed to talk. I blinked at him, and I knew he understood.

"Is there anything else?" Ivy asked, reaching into the bowl.

"That's the last of the meat," I said. "And the potatoes."

"There's never enough food anymore," she said, falling back in her chair. Her voice crackled as if she was going to cry. "I'm so hungry all the time."

"The Farthers eat most of it," I said. "And we have an extra mouth to feed now."

Everiss turned her head and fiddled with a tendril of hair. Jonn's mouth tightened. "Lia—"

"Maybe I should start going to the school in town," Ivy interrupted.

"What?" I gaped at her.

She lifted her chin. "They'll give us food."

"No. Absolutely not. They brainwash the students there."

"I'm not stupid," she said. "I know they teach lies. I won't believe them. I won't listen."

"Ivy—"

"I don't want to starve to death!" she burst out. "Do you?"

I flinched. Jonn and I looked at each other. He pressed his lips together and didn't speak.

"I'll go into the woods tomorrow, check the traps again," I said finally, with a sigh. "You can find more berries—"

"It's never enough," she said. Her voice was a whisper, full of dread and strong with certainty. Something twisted in the pit of my stomach, because she was right. It wasn't ever enough. We needed more food. Still, she couldn't go to Raine's military Farther school. She couldn't. Just the thought made bile rise in my throat.

Everiss sat very still through the entire conversation. Her mouth trembled, and her hands looked small and fragile in her lap. Slowly, involuntarily, she raised one to rub her shoulder where she'd been shot a few weeks ago. The silence shivered and stretched until I could barely stand it. Finally, Ivy rose and reached for the plates. "I'll do the dishes," she announced, her tone subdued.

Everiss grabbed the cups. "I'll help you." She crossed the room after my sister without looking at either of us. I saw the blush staining the back of her neck. She was ashamed that she was eating our food.

Jonn and I waited until they'd moved into the kitchen.

"Jonn," I said. "She can't do it. She can't go to that Farther school. She's so impressionable, what if they turn her into one of them? What if they infiltrate her mind with their lies?"

He gazed at me, his expression shrewd. "But what if she's right? What if we need this?"

"We'll find food somehow," I said. "Some other way. I'll learn to hunt. I'll trap more. I'll speak to Ann—"

"Our sister has grown up in the last month," he said. "She's been through a great deal, and she's learned."

"She's still too young." I knotted my hands into fists and stared at them. Atticus, our lack of food, my sister's safety, Everiss...everything. My eyes burned, and my chest squeezed tight.

"What is it?" he murmured. "You're upset. More Watchers in the woods?"

I struggled to find a response, but nothing came. I just felt unsettled. Uneasy. It was this bad feeling I sensed between Adam and Atticus, and the secrecy involved. But I couldn't tell him about it, not yet. I just shook my head.

"How is the search coming?" I asked, glancing at the stack of journals and papers beside the table.

Jonn brushed a few crumbs from the table with his hand. He took his time answering. "I believe Da included instructions about how to use the PLD in one of his journals, just as he included clues about where to find it in the riddles he told us. But like I said before, I don't know how to unravel the code in what he's written. There are a few cryptic mentions of a key to decoding the journals, but I don't know where it might be. It's missing."

Just as Adam had suspected.

"Do you think perhaps the Mayor has it? If Da was carrying it when he was shot, and Cole—"

"Not the Mayor," I said. "Not anymore."

I needed to pay Korr's private quarters a visit.

SIX

MY HEAD ACHED and my muscles burned from the previous day's physical exertion as I headed for the village the next morning. The unease I'd felt last night had not dissipated with sleep. Bad feelings still lapped at the edges of my mind, and worry gnawed a hole in my stomach, but I pushed the feelings away. I had other things to deal with besides the mess of feelings stewing in my chest. I used to be sensible, hardened, practical. Now look at me. I was practically a sniveling mess— worrying about Adam, worrying about Jonn and Everiss, worrying about everything and everyone. Worry, worry, worry. Was this what caring did to people? It made me feel weak.

Grinding my teeth together, I moved faster down the path. The edges of my cloak brushed the snow blossoms that lined the path. The sack of quota thumped against my shoulder, and a cool wind teased my face and played with the edges of my cloak. Everywhere, the forest was dripping.

I felt restless. The weather made my blood itch with longing, although I didn't know what that longing might be. I thought about the PLD and what we planned to do with it. Could we really find Gabe? Just thinking his name made my chest simmer with anxious anticipation. We didn't know where the gate had taken them, only that they were all together wherever they were. Would he want to come back? Would he want me?

The last thought cropped up unbidden, and I stopped on the path.

Gabe and I...we had never declared anything regarding our feelings. We'd known from the start that our love was doomed, that he must leave, that I was a Frost dweller and he was a Farther and that those two things were as compatible as fire and water. We had loved fiercely with the full knowledge that every moment was a stolen one and that every word might be the last. I didn't regret it, either. Knowing Gabe, and caring for him, had awakened a fire in me that had burned into a beacon of life, incinerating my reluctance and fear in the flames of justice and passion.

I wasn't sorry I'd loved him.

But I didn't know how I felt now, either. Could I love him again? Could he still love me?

Would he want to be with me?

Adam clearly seemed to think so, which was why he refused to address the feelings between us. And I...I didn't know what I thought, or what I wanted. Everything was in a muddle in my head.

I shook my head and began walking again. This was silly. It wasn't as if Gabe was standing before me, offering marriage. I had no idea what he wanted. And this pining...it was useless. I had other things to worry about. Korr. Blackcoats. Everiss. Raine. And now, Atticus.

Yanking my attention to more pressing matters, I mulled over Adam's words about our new Thorns leader as I turned the corner of the path and entered the Cages. There was something between them, something Adam didn't want to admit. It made my stomach twist with apprehension. I didn't like being in the dark like this—how was I supposed to know what to do if Adam wouldn't let me in?

I entered the village and headed through the cobbled streets for the quota yard. The sound of chanting drifted on the wind as I passed the new school, and a shudder ran down my spine. Through the windows, I saw the children in their uniforms, like little rows of Farther soldiers decked out in matching gray and brass. Their mouths moved in unison as they intoned facts about Aeralis, and the Farther teacher, a thin man with a withered neck and piercing black eyes, paced down one of the aisles. He brandished a ruler in his hand like a weapon. One of the children looked out the window and saw me. I put my head down and hurried on.

Lines filled the quota yard already. Villagers holding firewood, cloth, and other goods shuffled their feet against the cold and tried not to make eye contact with the soldiers as they delivered their bundles of supplies to the quota master and received their allotments of food in return. Across the yard, I spotted Adam Brewer, but he didn't acknowledge me. The wind stirred his dark hair across his eyes, and I bit my lip as something painful panged deep in the pit of my stomach. He wasn't handsome, not by any objective standard, but the way he moved and spoke and smiled—the way he slid his gaze over me—lit my blood on fire whenever I caught sight of him.

Jonn needed to speak with him. I dared not approach Adam in the village, not like this, but I could pass him a signal. I curled my fingers into a crooked shape of a Y and flashed them against my cloak. Had he seen it? I couldn't tell—Adam's expression never changed. He slipped away into the crowd, and I moved forward in line and gave my quota to the quota master while the Farther soldiers flanking him watched.

I didn't see Ann's red cloak and hood anywhere. Usually, the bright splash of color stood out against the grays and blues like a drop of blood on a snow blossom, but today she was missing. Apprehension stirred in my stomach, but I shoved the sensation away. She didn't meet me every time I came to the village for quota delivery or Assembly. She was fine. She was just busy—or late.

Still, I couldn't shake the gnawing worry. So after I'd turned over the yarn to the quota master and received our pitifully small sack of supplies in return, I turned left and headed for the hill in the center of the village instead of the gate to the Frost.

The boards of the Mayor's house gleamed the color of bleached bone in the pale sunlight, and dagger-like icicles glittered along the roof. Even the footprints left by soldiers' boots looked like ugly scars. Everything about the house felt dangerous now.

I held my breath as I climbed the back steps and rapped three times on the door.

A servant opened it. She regarded me with a frown. "Yes?"

The password. Ann would recognize it and know I needed to see her. "I—I need to show Ann Mayor some yarn," I said. "I'm Lia Weaver."

The girl shook her head. "I'm sorry, but she cannot see you now. You'll have to come back." She shut the door in my face.

I knocked again, and this time when the girl opened the door, I pushed against it.

"Hey!" She threw up an arm to block me.

"I have something to tell Ann Mayor. She will be angry when she finds out that you wouldn't—"

"Let the girl in," a voice purred, and I froze.

Korr.

The servant girl's face smoothed, and she stepped back, allowing me entrance. I didn't dare run. I crossed the threshold. My pulse hammered in my throat and my palms tingled with sudden sweat.

The young nobleman stood in the hall. He was tall, with striking black hair and eyes. His face was almost identical to Gabe's, except his was crueler, and the expression he wore was far more cunning.

He was Gabe's brother, and my enemy.

"Lia Weaver," he said, his tone a threat sheathed in pleasantries. "What brings you here?"

"I was looking for Ann," I said.

"Ah, she's your friend, isn't she? It's a rather fascinating connection. The penniless Weaver and the wealthy Mayor girl."

"I have things to give her. She needs yarn." I said it frostily.

He dimpled. "Of course. But Ann is not here at the moment."

An idea took hold in my brain. A desperate, wild, crazy idea.

"I have something you might want to discuss," I said to him. "In your private rooms."

"Oh?" One perfectly manicured eyebrow lifted skeptically. He smirked at me. "'Discuss?'"

My heart was pounding. My breath caught in my throat. I ignored his suggestive comment and rasped the words. "It concerns a young man named Gabe."

Korr straightened at the mention of his brother's name. His arms dropped to his sides, and he shot a look at the maid that clearly meant she was dismissed. She scurried away, and he beckoned to me with one crisp snap of his fingers. "Come."

I followed him up the stairs and down the hall. Was I utterly mad? What had possessed me to do this?

This gamble had to pay off.

I was light-headed as he let me into the room. The walls were a dark maroon, and striped gold paper covered the wall behind the massive bed. A writing desk strewn with papers stood beside a window framed by drooping velvet curtains. I blinked at the furnishings. Where had all this come from? It looked fit for a palace.

"I had these things imported from Aeralis," Korr said, noting my astonishment. "I couldn't very well live in squalor, could I?" But he didn't wait for whatever response I might have had to that statement. He shut the door and turned a key in the lock. The sinister click reverberated in my ears, and I shivered. Korr pocketed the key and paced to the window. He stared through the frosted pane at the street below. The sunlight lit the edges of his hair and made him look like a devil.

"Now," he said, his voice little more than a growl. "Tell me what you know about this Gabe."

I licked my lips to moisten them. I edged toward the writing table. "He came through here a few months ago. He was a fugitive. The Farther soldiers were looking for him. I—I saw him." I took another step toward the table. My gaze fell on a wrinkled sheet of paper peeking out from beneath the others. My heart skipped a beat when I realized it was my father's handwriting. Did Korr know what this was? Scribbles covered it, familiar-looking scribbles. A circle. Numbers, letters. A string of them, all together. I tried to commit them to memory.

"Yes," Korr said, swinging around to face me. "I know—the bracelet you wear was his."

I dropped my eyes to the piece on my hand. I'd found it after Gabe had left and I'd wore it to remind myself of him. I hadn't realized anyone had noticed it. It was just a plain thing.

He turned back to the window. I edged closer to the desk and scanned the paper. It was a key for some kind of code, perhaps?

"Yes," I said. "I found him in the woods and I gave him shelter in my barn."

Korr's eyebrows shot up. "And where is he now?"

"I don't know." And it was true. I said the words simply, honestly.

Korr was silent. Sweat beaded on my forehead as I hastily committed the scribbles on the paper to memory. I didn't dare try to touch it...

"You may go," he said finally.

"I—"

"Go!"

I went.

~

I burst into the farmhouse, startling Jonn. I grabbed the nearest paper on the table and plucked the pencil from his hand. Bending over it, I began to empty my head of the string of numbers and letters I'd memorized in Korr's room.

"Hey!" my brother yelped. "What are you doing?"

Ivy and Everiss looked up from their places by the fire. Ivy hurried over, curious. I ignored them all and kept writing. I had to get all this right before I forgot everything.

When I'd finished, I thrust the paper in Jonn's face. "Here."

"What's that?" Ivy demanded.

Jonn looked from the scribbles to my face, his eyes wide.

"It's the key to decode the journals." He grabbed the paper and flattened it across the table in front of him. He fumbled for the first journal in the stack at his elbow and flipped it open, mumbling under his breath.

"Where did you find that?" Ivy said, but I shook my head and steered her back to the fire. We needed to let our brother work.

Hours passed. Impatience simmered in my blood as I occupied my fingers with weaving. Would this really help Jonn figure out how to operate the PLD? Had Korr suspected anything? What would he do with the knowledge I'd given him, the knowledge that I'd seen Gabe? Had my gamble been worth it?

Finally, Jonn dropped his pencil with a sigh. "Lia," he whispered, and I set aside the yarn and strode across the room to his side. Before him lay a paper with a set of instructions.

"Is that it?"

"Not yet. But it's a step in the right direction."

"Well?" I demanded. "What now?"

"I need to go to Echlos," Jonn said.

SEVEN

"ARE YOU SURE he's strong enough to make the trip?" Adam asked. Our footsteps crunched as we moved through the forest, and all around us bits of snow drifted down like feathers. The fading light filled the Frost with a bluish glow as darkness fell, and ahead, I saw the glint of metal. One of my father's traps.

"Jonn is stronger than anyone realizes," I said firmly, but inside I worried. What about his seizures, his fevers? But he'd been adamant. "He said he must go. He said he has only clues, but he'll know the hiding place when he sees it. He isn't simply looking for an adventure."

"I trust your brother means what he says," Adam said.

"This might be the only way."

He turned to study my face for a moment. "All right," he said. "We'll take him together."

Silence fell between us as we continued on.

"Is Atticus...has he found a place to stay?" I asked, brushing a strand of hair from my eyes. I stepped over a fallen log after Adam.

"Yes. He's settled in." That seemed to be all Adam wanted to say on the subject.

I ducked beneath a branch and stepped over a cluster of icy stones. "It seems odd that he would be assigned here when he knows nothing of the Frost."

Adam just looked at me.

"Sometimes I think you Thorns operatives are over-enamored with secrecy," I muttered. "Not knowing every other agent in the region is one thing. Refusing to tell me what's going on with things that concern me is another."

"The Trio knows what they're doing. We just have to follow orders."

"The Trio?" For some reason, the name was oddly familiar to me, but I couldn't place where I'd heard it.

"The Trio is what we call the group of Thorns leaders—three men or women who control everything the organization does. Their identities are shrouded in complete secrecy, and not even the rest of the organization knows their names or faces. They are the most hunted individuals in Aeralis, and they remain in hiding always."

I remembered—Atticus had mentioned them in the barn. The way he'd said the word...he'd used it like a weapon. I frowned.

"So the Trio made the choice to send him here?"

"Yes," Adam said. "They know what they're doing. We just have to trust the plan."

But I wasn't sure that I did.

~

79

We rode the horses into the Frost the next afternoon. Jonn sat behind me on the gelding that I jokingly referred to as Officer Raine, and Adam rode the mare. The snow absorbed the sound of the hoofbeats, and silence shrouded us as it always did when venturing into the Frost. Unease simmered in my stomach as we put more distance between ourselves and the farm. I hadn't told Everiss anything about where we were going or what we were up to, but obviously Jonn never left the house, so she couldn't help but notice and wonder. Ivy was missing again, a pattern which was beginning to concern me. I made a mental note to talk to her about it later.

The horses crested the final hill and the forest fell away. A field of snow and ice stretched before us to the river, and the mountains rose up to the sky in the distance in a haze of purple. "Echlos," Adam said under his breath.

"I don't see anything..." Jonn began, his face knit with confusion.

"Just wait," I said. I kicked the gelding into a trot as we crossed the field.

"Lia, I don't...*oh.*" Jonn's fingers tightened with astonishment on my shoulders as the shield shimmered and evaporated, revealing the ancient buildings. Smooth, rounded white roofs rose like giant eggshells from the ground. Vines and trees crowded the architecture and choked the dark hole that used to be the door.

We dismounted. Adam pulled Jonn off the horse with a grunt and carried him bride-style. I followed, watching them both for any signs of fatigue. Jonn slung an arm around Adam's neck and twisted around, trying to see everything as we approached the ruins.

"This is incredible," he murmured again and again, staring at the sloping roofs, the crumbling columns, and the iridescent shimmer of the visible walls.

"Wait till you see inside," I said.

We entered the gaping hole that used to be the entrance and descended the staircase. Adam went first, still carrying Jonn. I paused before entering and took a deep breath. The closeness of the tunnels always made my throat squeeze and my heart beat too fast.

After I'd taken a moment to clear my head and steel my nerves, I stepped after them into the darkness. The scent of dusty air met my nose, and a shiver ran up my spine at the memories that filled my head. *Gabe. Lantern-light dancing on the ground. Adam and his brother, their faces grim and unmoving as they slipped through the depths ahead of us...*

Jonn's voice echoed ahead of me, around a corner. "Unbelievable."

I hurried to join them. They were by the curving staircase. Adam had set Jonn down, and he was staring up at the ceiling and the lights that had come on, flickering like captured lightning.

"Well," I said, after we'd stood in silence a moment. "What now?"

My brother looked down the corridor, and he sighed as if gathering strength for an arduous task. "Take me to the gate."

We made the climb into the bowels of the ruins slowly, taking care with the hundreds of stairs and ramps strewn with dirt and debris. Each step carried a memory of the last night I'd made this journey, almost four months ago now. Every time I blinked, I saw Gabe. My breathing rasped in my lungs and my eyes burned at the feelings that washed over me. But I pushed them away. Now was not the time to get emotional.

Finally, we reached the room where the gate waited.

Light broke over us as we stepped through the gaping hole where a massive door had once been. The ceiling stretched up to a point hundreds of feet away, and sunlight flooded down through a splintered gap in the roof. Snow and ice covered the stone floor, and dead vines dangled in brown strands from scaffolding-like structures that crowded the corners and walls of the room. Far away, through the hole in the roof, I could see a patch of blue sky and wisps of storm clouds. At the far end of the room, the gate waited for us like the blind eye of a sleeping monster, illuminated by daylight and flecked with dappled shadow. I shivered as the wind rushed through the hole and across our bare faces.

"This is it," Adam said, and his voice was just a whisper in the vastness of the room.

Jonn looked up, and his throat bobbed as he swallowed. He turned his head, drinking in the sight, and I stared along with him. "Take me closer, please."

Our footsteps scuffled as we crossed the chamber. The wind rustled across the ice and made the metal structures creak and groan. Adam scanned the room with the eye of a hunter looking for other hunters, and Jonn craned his neck and muttered under his breath, absorbed in a stream of symbols along the wall.

But I couldn't take my eyes off the portal as we drew closer.

Before, I'd only seen the gate in the dead of night, the same night we'd delivered Gabe to safety months ago. I'd been back to Echlos since, but never to the portal itself. It looked different now, illuminated by sunlight and flickering shadow. Faded, almost dismal. The gray circle was splattered with stains from hundreds of years of snow and ice, and dried lichen clung to the sides. The faintest outline of markings straggled up one side like the faded remnants of bird droppings. They looked as though they'd once been words, but whatever they had said had been scraped away by the elements long ago.

A lump filled my throat. The gate looked dead now. Impotent. Nothing but a round, flat piece of metal surrounded by ruins. I remembered how it'd sprang to life, how the air had hummed, how the snow around had crackled with power. I remembered the way the edges had closed around Gabe like a mouth around a morsel of food.

Where did this gate lead? Where had it taken him? And how in the world were we supposed to find him and the others to bring them back?

Jonn craned his neck as we drew closer. His eyes played over the gate and the panels that flanked it. He seemed to be searching for something. His fingers brushed the air as he gestured to the left, at one of the walls. "There, please."

Adam carried him forward, and Jonn reached out one hand to touch the stone.

"Here," he murmured to himself, looking for something. "No...wait. Here."

More etchings covered this wall, these ones symbols that made no sense. A figure. A triangle. Something that looked like raindrops.

Jonn frowned. His eyebrows pulled together in a dark line, and he traced the triangle with his hand. "There should be something here," he said.

"Something?" I asked, but he didn't answer me.

"A little more to the left, please," he said.

Adam stepped farther down the wall, a few paces more past the portal. Jonn gazed up at the vast stretch of gray stone and rusted metal. He muttered under his breath and reached out again. I saw another symbol, a fainter one.

I watched, astonished, as he pressed his palm against the wall. A panel flipped open, and something tumbled out and bounced on the ground with a clatter. I gasped.

Adam crouched and set Jonn down on the floor with a groan. He picked up the fallen object and turned it over in his hands—a flat box, tightly sealed. Sunlight glinted off the metal edge and hurt my eyes.

"What is this?" I asked.

"Another, final journal. The location was described in the code Da left," Jonn said. He was breathless. "The location by the gate...the symbols on the wall...this was all left for someone to find."

"Us?"

"Maybe."

He took the box from Adam and felt across the top. There was a click, and the top flipped open. He pulled out a sheaf of papers and a folded-up journal, and then he met my eyes with a delighted smile.

"I think we just found our instructions."

~

Jonn muttered to himself under his breath and thumbed through the journal the entire way back to the farm. The journal was badly torn and burned in places, as if it had been carried through a war zone. Whole sections were missing.

"Will it be of any use to you?" I asked.

Jonn waved a hand at me that meant *yes*...or *shut up*...it was hard to tell.

When we reached the house again, Adam carried Jonn inside while I stabled the animals. When I emerged from the barn, he was waiting for me on the porch of the farmhouse, his hands tucked in his pockets and the wind blowing his hair into his eyes.

"If what your brother found is what he thinks it is..."

"We'll be able to find them," I finished.

"Yes."

When we reached the door, he touched my elbow. I felt the heat of his fingers through my clothing, and the place where he touched me burned. I dragged my eyes up to meet his.

"I need to speak with Jonn alone," he said, giving me a grim and apologetic smile.

"Oh." I took a step back and fumbled with my cloak. "Of course." Confusion swam in my chest, along with a trace of hurt. Weren't we all in this mission together? But I pushed the emotions away. I was a Thorns agent, not a silly little girl who pouted a kept secret.

"I'll be in the barn if you need me," I said.

"Thank you." He went into the house, and I stood on the stoop and stared at the door while the wind teased my hair and blew its chilly breath beneath the edges of my cloak.

I turned and slogged through the snow to the barn.

~

Adam found me later. I was brushing the horses with short, firm strokes. The smell of leather and old hay filled my nostrils, but I smelled pine and ice and knew he was behind me before he spoke.

"Have you finished your business with my brother?" I asked, without turning around.

"I have." He spoke calmly, gravely. There was a distance between us, and it both puzzled and distressed me. I turned.

"Adam—"

"There are things that cannot be shared with you, Lia. I've received orders that the contents of the journal we discovered are to be kept secret. Only Jonn and his superior—me—and my superior are to know them. I am sorry."

"Don't be sorry," I said. "It's how things must be. It might be a little odd, not being able to talk with him about it as we've been doing, but I understand."

The muscles in his jaw relaxed slightly at my words, and the lines on his forehead eased. "I'm pleased that you understand."

He was using formality between us like a shield. I made a noise of frustration in my throat and reached for the brush again. He covered my hand with his, and I stared at it.

"Lia—"

The barn door burst open and my sister stumbled in. "Lia," she gasped. "Come quickly."

Adam pulled his hand from mine as we both turned. "What is it?"

"Jonn's having a seizure! It's a bad one."

Seizure. The word struck me like a stone. I picked up my skirts without another word and ran for the house.

My brother lay on the floor of the main room, convulsing. His eyes were white in his head and froth ran from his lips. Everiss crouched beside him, her hands fluttering over his chest, and when she saw me she scrambled up. "Lia! Quick!"

"It's all right," I said, speaking firmly. "Put a blanket in his mouth—sometimes he bites his tongue. Ivy, grab the quilts. Let's just keep him warm until it passes."

I didn't miss the fear flashing in Everiss's eyes as she hurried to do what I'd ordered. Her hands shook as she fumbled with one of the blankets that had been thrown across the back of Jonn's chair. I knelt beside my brother and took his hand. His fingers were twisted in a gnarled claw of a shape, and I rubbed them. "It's all right, brother," I murmured.

Adam came in and shut the door behind him. He knelt beside me and didn't say anything, but his presence comforted me.

Finally, the seizure abated. My brother lay still, his arms and legs limp, his mouth slack. I breathed out in relief. "Can you help me carry him to the bedroom?"

Adam scooped Jonn up like he was just a bag of goose down and took him to my parents' bedroom. He laid Jonn on the bed and I covered him with a quilt. Everiss and Ivy hovered in the doorway, their eyes wide.

"He's fine," I assured Everiss, who looked ready to faint. "Sometimes he has episodes like this, but they always pass. Do we have anything we can make soup with? He'll be hungry when he wakes."

"I'll heat the water," Ivy volunteered. She disappeared into the main room. Everiss went to the bed and stood beside Jonn, gazing down at his sleeping face.

Adam and I went out to the fireside.

"Have you ever called the Healer?" he asked.

"Garrett Healer has seen him, as has his daughter, Brenna Healer. They could do nothing for him. There was another Healer, a traveling one who roamed the Frost between villages, and he described a procedure that he'd heard of in Aeralis that might help. Of course, such hope is impossible for us."

"Maybe if—"

I lifted my head, and my eyes narrowed. Adam fell silent.

"There are no maybes. There is nothing to be done. I will not entertain foolish notions about maybe. It will get Ivy's hopes up, nothing more."

Adam ran one finger up and down the edge of his cloak. He didn't speak.

"He's working too hard," I said, standing and going to the table where the journals were spread in a semicircle. "The trip to Echlos must have exhausted him. That and the lack of food...maybe he should be off this mission."

"Don't coddle him. He's part of the Thorns now. He has a job to do, the same as you and me. You know that."

"Lia," a voice called weakly from the bedroom.

I hurried to his side with Ivy at my heels. Adam stayed by the fire, watching the flames. Everiss moved back to give us space, and I dropped to my knees at my brother's side and brushed a few damp strands of hair from his forehead. "How do you feel?"

His lips quirked in a smile. "Stupid," he rasped. "I haven't had a bad episode in years and now..."

"You're pushing yourself too hard."

His eyes flickered. He struggled to sit up. "Is Adam still here?"

"Jonn..."

He turned his head and gazed straight into my eyes. A vein in his neck pulsed, and he gritted his teeth. "Don't."

A pang shot through me at his tone. I understood. I dropped my hand and climbed to my feet. "I'll get him." I gave Everiss and Ivy a look as I left the room, and they followed me without speaking. "He wants to speak with you," I told Adam, my words terse, and then I stepped into the kitchen and banged the pans around for a bit as my anger settled.

The girls busied themselves with the little food we had left. The soup bubbled and simmered on the stove, and when it was hot enough, Ivy ladled it into bowls. I didn't miss the way her hands trembled.

"Shall I take one to Jonn?" she asked me, licking her lips and stealing a look at Everiss as if seeking solidarity against the heat of my anger.

"Give them a minute," I barked, flicking my gaze at the door, which Adam had shut behind him.

I couldn't protect him. Every fiber of my being ached to, but he wasn't going to let me. I knew I had to acquiesce. I had to step back and let it go.

90

Finally, Adam emerged. His dark gaze tangled with mine, but he didn't let it linger there. He crossed the room and let himself out into the cold.

My chest felt hollow. I stood still for a moment, absorbing the feeling and struggling to keep my face composed. I heard Jonn's voice over the sound of the fire on the hearth and the clank of dishes behind me. I went into the room again.

"Bring me the journal, please," he said. "The one we found at Echlos."

His eyelids fluttered with exhaustion, and his fingers shivered against the blankets. I hesitated. Something cold and hard and dread-shaped knotted in the pit of my stomach.

"Please. Lia," he said. "I have things I have to do before I can sleep."

"You need to rest."

"Don't treat me like a child!" The words cut through the air like a knife. I flinched. "Don't," he said, softer now. "Don't do that to me. Give me some dignity, sister."

My cheeks flushed, and I whirled to fetch him the journals. I put the newest one on the top of the stack.

"Thank you," he breathed, when I'd deposited them on the bed beside his hand. He touched his fingertips to the paper and then lifted his face toward me. "I'm sorry...I'm very tired. I didn't mean it."

"No, you're right. I'm sorry."

We shared a terse smile, and then he lifted one of the books with a look that said he wanted to be alone. I slipped out and shut the door. I slumped against it and pressed a hand over my eyes.

I wanted to talk to Adam, but he'd already left...and perhaps I just needed to think about this myself.

"Will he be all right?" Everiss asked from across the room.

"He'll be fine," I said. "He just needs rest."

But I wasn't sure I believed my own words.

EIGHT

THE NEXT MORNING, Jonn was awake and pouring over the journal we'd found in Echlos even though his face was still pale and his hands trembled. Everiss had slept by the fire in his place. Ivy was gone again to find berries, they told me.

Unease churned in my stomach. Jonn wasn't better yet. Atticus still concerned me. And I was worried about Ann. I hadn't seen her in days.

"I have to go into the village today," I told Everiss. "Keep Jonn quiet and try to keep him from getting up. Feed him soup and milk. I'll bring back some herbs that always calm him."

She nodded at my instructions and swallowed hard. Her lip trembled as she glanced toward the closed bedroom door. "Will he have another episode, do you think?"

"I don't think so, but I can't be sure. So try to keep him calm and comfortable until I get back."

It was the most cordial conversation we'd had since she'd come to stay with us. Jonn's injuries had knit us together in a most unexpected way, but I didn't have time to ponder it. I needed to fetch the herbs, deliver my quota, and see if Ann was all right. I hadn't laid eyes on her in days. "I'll be back shortly," I said, and left for the village.

The sky was pale blue and pebbled with clouds. Snow dripped from the trees and ice leaked everywhere. When I reached the village, the streets ran wet with weeping sludge. I hurried through the streets for the market, where I always traded bits of yarn for the herbs I needed.

Old woman Tanna peered at me shrewdly. "Yarn for herbs?"

"Yes," I said, impatient. "Just as always."

"Can't," the woman said, turning her head to cough into her sleeve. "Food only."

"I don't have any food to spare."

She gazed at me with watery eyes. "Then no herbs."

Turning on my heel, I stalked away before I said or did anything rash. My blood flamed with anger, but I knew she had to look out for herself, too. She needed to eat as much as anyone, but that thought didn't make the lack of medicine for my brother any less bitter.

I needed to see Ann. Maybe she could do something to help us. I lifted my gaze to the Mayor's house, white and cold in the sunlight at the top of the hill. My heart clenched with sudden foreboding. I drew in a breath and began to head toward it.

A hand snagged my arm, and I was wrenched into an alley and pressed up against a wall. Dark eyes gazed into mine. Adam.

"Brewer—what—?"

He released me but didn't step back. "Where are you going?"

"To speak with my best friend." I straightened my cloak and glared at him. The anger swirled in me, making me irritable and bold. "Why are you suddenly snatching people out of the street? You're going to attract unwanted attention."

Adam folded his arms. "You should expect to see less of Ann for a while. She's on a mission."

"A mission?" My brow furrowed. "On your orders?"

"Not mine," he said. "Atticus's."

"What mission? Where is she?"

"It involves...Korr."

I waited for him to explain further, but he didn't. A poisonous sensation pooled in my chest. He was going to keep this secret. "Is she all right, at least?"

"She's fine," he said. "She has her orders."

I ran an eye over him. He wasn't wearing his usual blue cloak, but a dark gray one. The clothes he wore beneath were black. "You are dressed differently."

"I have a mission of my own."

He didn't tell me more. My mouth twisted in a frown.

Before I could ask, he was slipping away, and I was left feeling hollow and cold.

~

95

When I arrived back at the farm, Everiss and Ivy were nowhere to be seen. The house smelled like wet wool and wood smoke, and the fire on the hearth had burned down to coals. Jonn was sitting at the table, flushed and glassy-eyed, surrounded by papers with his notes scribbled across them. The journal from Echlos lay in his lap. The PLD lay beside his left hand, the wires spread out like the tentacles of an alien creature.

Frustration flared in my chest. I shut the door hard and yanked off my cloak. "What are you doing up?"

"I did it," he said. The words burst out of him all at once, shutting me up.

"What?"

"I did it," he repeated. An exhausted smile hovered at the edges of his mouth but didn't quite land. "The journal...I deciphered how to use the PLD. The mission can move forward. We can bring them back." He dragged in a deep breath. "You have to signal Adam. I have to speak to him at once."

A tornado of emotion filled me—relief, excitement, dread. We could go through the portal now. This was it. I stood very still, staring at him.

"Did you hear me?" He seemed dazed. Whether it was from happiness or exhaustion, I couldn't tell.

"Let's get you back to bed," was all I could think to say.

"Lia..."

"I'll put out the lantern," I promised. "Now come on."

Before he let me help him back to bed, he scooped up the journal and his papers and clutched them to his chest. I tried to take them and he grabbed my wrist.

"It's my mission," he said. "Sorry, Lia. I'm not supposed to show anyone else except Adam."

I bit my tongue and stepped back, letting go of the papers. We shared this mission. There shouldn't be this secrecy between us. This was all Atticus's doing, and I hated it.

After I'd helped him to lie down, I went into the kitchen to scrape together some dinner. When I opened the cupboards, my stomach somersaulted. They were completely bare. I quickly catalogued the supplies in the barn in my head—we had a few barrels of dried apples, turnips for the cow...but we'd been dipping into them. They were already low. We had Everiss to feed now, and there hadn't been enough as it was.

The front door opened and shut. Ivy appeared in the hall, her nose red from the cold and her cheeks pale.

"Where's Everiss?" I asked.

"In the barn, finishing the chores. She felt strong enough today."

"And where have you been?" I was too tired, too defeated to be angry. I practically whispered the words.

My sister stood with her hands behind her back, chewing her lip.

"Berries?" I guessed, and a flicker of hope flared in me. It would be something, as pitiful as that something might be.

"No."

"What, then? I came home and Jonn was here by himself, working too hard as usual, and—"

"I signed up for the Farther school," she blurted out.

My mouth dropped open.

"There was no food—I didn't know what to do, and you were gone, and I've probably picked every berry between here and Aeralis, and we're all so hungry all the time. So I—I just went and did it." She lifted her arm, and I saw the bag she'd been holding behind her back. "They give you food just for putting your name on the list, did you know that? I start tomorrow."

"No," I said, desperate. Not at that horrible school where the children chanted in unison about the virtues of the Farther dictator.

"I have to," Ivy insisted. "We need food. In case you hadn't noticed, we're starving to death!"

"I'll check the traps again...I'll talk to Ann..."

"You have your contributions to the welfare of this family," she said. "Now let me have mine."

~

Adam came to the house later that night, after I put out the lantern. I let him in without a word, and pointed him toward the bedroom where Jonn was resting. I sat at the table and stared at the shut door while they conversed quietly on the other side. Everiss slept by the fire and Ivy was upstairs in the loft. The fire crackled, and the wind moaned around the corners of the house and through the seams of the windowpanes. Snow fell softly, feather-light.

The bedroom door opened and closed, and Adam crossed the room and sank into one of the chairs beside me and put his chin in his hand.

"Well?" I asked.

"He's done it."

We sat together silently for a moment, drinking that thought in.

I sighed. "I'm frightened."

"Me too," he admitted.

I looked at him in surprise, but he didn't acknowledge me. He just looked at the fire. "Now what?" I asked after another stretch of silence.

Adam ran one finger along the edge of the table, dusting away a speck of a crumb. "You'll have to continue your training without me for a while, but I don't want you to slack off. You can use my family's barn to do the exercises I taught you, of course—"

"Wait," I interrupted. "What are you talking about?"

"I'm the one who's going to go," he said. "I have to go through the portal to get them."

I stared at him. How had I not realized? I supposed I just hadn't thought about it. Of course someone would have to go. Of course that someone would be Adam, the strongest and most experienced among us.

Still, the admission stunned me.

"How long will you be gone?"

A muscle in his jaw jumped. "It should be a few weeks at least until anyone is able to return."

"A few weeks?"

"According to what Jonn has discovered from the journals, the portal operates on very specific principles of space and time. We'll have to coordinate and utilize exact dates for any organized return to this specific place, and these times occur only at certain intervals. Once I travel to where the fugitives are, we'll have to wait in order to return at the right location. It won't be available immediately unless I left as soon as I arrived, which I can't count on. It may take time to find and organize them all."

I nodded, absorbing this information. "So portal travel is like a Farther train or airship, with certain departure times?"

"A little," he said.

Coldness seeped through me. I didn't want to say aloud how much I would miss him, or how vulnerable we'd feel with him gone. We'd come to depend on his presence heavily, and the truth of it was now staring me starkly in the face. I shivered and clasped my arms around me, but I didn't say anything. I had to be strong. I had to be Lia Weaver, invincible and unemotional, not this sopping mess of worry and concern that I'd become.

I thought of Gabe—his face had grown almost hazy in my mind over the last few months—and my heart twisted. I felt pulled in two. I didn't want Adam to go...but I wanted Gabe to come back, even with as much as I feared and dreaded seeing him again, because I didn't know where we stood.

Adam stood. "I should go. I need to meet with Atticus tonight to discuss what must be done, and then I have other places to be."

"Other missions?" I asked lightly.

He hesitated a long moment, as if he had something he wanted to say. "There's always another mission," he said finally. It was a non-answer, and I felt the sting of that keenly. He was cutting me out again, and it hurt. "Be well, Lia Weaver. The mission begins tomorrow, but I'll see you again soon. Stay strong. I..."

He didn't finish the thought.

I raised my gaze to his.

He hesitated, then reached out and brushed his fingers across my cheek. The touch of his hand sent a tremble through me. His eyes blazed, but he didn't speak. He turned to go.

My heart hammered. *Tomorrow.*

"Wait. Adam?"

He stopped by the door, his hand resting against the frame. He didn't turn back.

I went to his side and lowered my voice. "I'm not happy about this—this secrecy. Do you think it really protects us? Or is it simply making us more vulnerable, more easily divided? It's one thing to keep some things secret to avoid giving up information when under torture. It's another thing to be so cut off from one another that we can't help each other when we need it."

His fingers drummed against the doorframe. "You don't understand. Atticus is—"

"Then help me understand."

He shook his head. "I really must go. We'll talk later."

"Adam..."

He touched a finger to my lips, silencing me, and then he went out into the night, leaving me standing there alone.

NINE

THE WALK TO the village the next morning crackled with unvoiced tension. Ivy kept pace with me, but her cloak fluttered pitifully in the wind, and her dark eyes looked huge in her face. She was nervous.

I was nervous, too. I didn't want to let her do this, and I still wasn't convinced that she had to, either. I would go to the Mayor's house, speak to Ann. Perhaps a servant position was open, one that could be paid in food...

There had to be *something.* Some other option.

Ivy aside, concern about the mission gnawed at my insides. I didn't know what was happening. I felt as though I were tiptoeing across ice, not knowing when or where it might crack.

"Don't worry about me," Ivy said at last. "I know how to take care of myself."

"I'm always going to worry," I told her. She rolled her eyes. I felt old. Motherish. Brittle with worry.

We came into sight of the Cage. Ivy shivered. I touched her shoulder once, she gave me a tremulous smile, and we entered the tunnel together. She left my side only when we reached the schoolhouse.

The others had already assembled, and already I could hear the sound of their chanting. A trickle of unease ran down my spine, but my sister was already slipping through the gate and up the path. I stared after her, helpless, and as soon as she'd vanished inside, I headed straight for the hill and the Mayor's house.

I needed to speak to Ann. Mission or not, it had been too many days since we'd spoken. I needed her help. I needed her friendship.

A servant answered my knock.

"I need to speak with Ann Mayor," I said as firmly as I could muster. "I have some yarn—"

"Can't," the servant said.

"She'll want to see me."

"That may be true, but Miss Ann isn't here." The servant began to close the door. I shoved my foot in the crack and thrust my face close to hers.

"What do you mean, she isn't here? Where is she? I can wait."

"She's in Astralux," the servant said. "With Lord Korr."

"Astralux?" *Korr?*

"The Aeralian capital." The servant said it in a clipped tone, as if I was an imbecile.

I was so stunned that she managed to push my foot away and close the door in my face. I stared at the knob, numb with shock, my mind spinning twenty directions at once.

Ann was in Astralux? The capital city of Aeralis? And she was there with Korr? As his prisoner? For some other reason altogether?

What was going on?

The secrets were getting out of control. I needed to speak to Adam.

~

I travelled straight from the village to the Brewer farm, and as I went, I considered every possibility. Had she journeyed there again with her father, perhaps? Was it possible she'd made the trip alone under some excuse of tourism? Was this about her mission?

Was this Atticus's doing?

I reached the Brewer farm and hurried straight to the barn. Adam should be there. If he wasn't, I could leave a message... I hadn't really thought any of this through. I was simply moving. I wrenched the door open and stopped.

Someone was there, but it wasn't Adam.

Atticus.

He stood facing the exercise ropes, his hands on his hips. He turned and saw me as I stepped inside, and his mouth curved in a careful smile that gave none of his thoughts away. "Lia Weaver," he said. "I'd so hoped that you'd come by today. We need to talk."

My heart flipped. "I need to speak with Adam Brewer."

"Brewer isn't here."

A little shiver raced through me. Not here. There was something so ominous about those words. "Then where is he?"

Atticus shook his head. "In the Thorns, every operative has his or her mission to accomplish. They don't concern themselves with others' business. Adam is on a *mission*. It is none of your concern."

All this secrecy was beginning to infuriate me. "That isn't how we did things before you came," I snapped.

His eyes narrowed. "I'm in charge now. We're doing things my way."

I shut my mouth and tried to be calm. He was right. I was being insubordinate.

"Listen to me, girl," Atticus said. "Right now, your concern is the PLD and Echlos. Your concern is those fugitives."

"Echlos? The fugitives? That is Adam's mission."

"Adam won't be able to complete his task regarding the PLD. He's occupied with something else." He paused. "I need you to do it instead."

I need you to do it. I blinked, swallowed, stuttered. I wasn't a seasoned operative. I wasn't the one who'd trained for this. "Me?"

He spoke crisply. "Yes. You are familiar with Echlos, you know something of the histories, you know several of the fugitives...you are the best one for the job."

"But my family..." I could not leave them for so long.

Atticus's eyes burned like black fire. "Your family— and everyone else in this town—are in great danger. The Farthers are slowly tightening their grip, and they won't

106

stop until everyone is crushed. You are a Thorns operative. You swore an oath to this cause. Now, are you going to do your duty?"

"Where is Adam?"

"He had other duties. He said you could handle this one. In fact, he insisted." Atticus paused.

"Oh," I said.

Atticus's eyes gleamed. "Was his faith in you misplaced?"

"No," I spoke firmly. "I can do it."

"Good. Now get home. Adam said your brother has the instructions. Get them from him, and meet me inside your barn tonight."

"Tonight?"

"There is no time to waste," he said. "Tonight must be the night. Now go!"

I stumbled for the door.

TEN

"YOU CAN'T BE serious," Jonn said after I'd delivered my news.

"I am." I felt frozen inside, calm to the point of deadness. My mind was focused solely on what I'd been told to do—get the PLD, get my instructions, meet Atticus in the barn—because otherwise I would crumble into a thousand pieces.

"And Adam—"

"Something happened. He isn't going to do it." My voice threatened to crack, but I pushed on. "And now Ann is in Astralux."

"Astralux?"

"Jonn. There's no time. We have to do this now." I spoke the words sharply, because otherwise I would tear into two. They had cut me out. They had gone on without me. It was done. Now, I had my duty to fulfill.

Jonn nodded. He gathered the journals and put them in a pile. Gingerly, he picked up the PLD case and handed it to me. His face was a mask of shock and confusion.

"You won't starve, brother," I said, desperate to reassure myself as much as him. "Ivy's at the Farther school, and without my mouth to feed, it's only three people. Ivy can take the quota into town, and Everiss can check the traps when she's strong enough, which should be any day now. You'll be fine until I get back."

He pursed his lips angrily. "You're sure you want to do this?"

"I *have* to do this," I said. "I'm in this all the way, just like you. And you've already risked your life and health. Look at what Ma and Da did. Now I have to do the same. Besides, there's no one else."

Adam and Ann were gone. I was alone in this. I was reeling.

"Are you sure—?"

"I'm sure."

He was silent a moment. Slowly, he nodded. "All right, then. Here are your instructions." Carefully, he explained exactly how to activate the device. "There isn't much time to go through after you've turned it on, and it will only fire once until the window of opportunity is open again," he said. "So don't do it until you're absolutely ready."

I nodded, committing everything he told me to memory. "Did you find all this in that journal?"

"Yes. Lia...do you know where you're going?"

I shrugged. "To wherever the gate leads."

"The journal...I know a little about where—"

"Don't bother telling me the details," I said. "There isn't time. I'll see it when I get there."

"Wait," Jonn said, before I could go. "I...there's something else."

"Hurry," I said. "I need to get going."

"This has nothing to do with the Thorns," he said. "This is something else." His tone was strange, and his eyes slid away from mine. He held out a sealed piece of paper. "There's someone who you need to find once you've traveled through the gate. He has something I need. You need to get him to give it to you."

"Who? What...?"

"It was in the journal. The one we found in Echlos," Jonn said. "Where you're going...I'm not sure, but I think there may be an important man there, Meridus Borde. I've read about him in the journal I found at Echlos. If you find him, give him this paper and tell him to follow the instructions exactly. It's very important, but I can't explain why. Do whatever you have to do to get it, Lia. Please. Trust me on this."

"All right," I said. "I will."

He nodded and sat back, exhausted. His face shone with sweat. "You'll say goodbye to Ivy before you leave?"

"I'll say goodbye," I promised.

~

Atticus sat cross-legged on the floor, smoking his pipe and waiting. He didn't rise when I entered. He took stock of me, noting the PLD case in my hands. I'd already slipped Jonn's paper into my pocket so he wouldn't see it and ask any questions.

A puff of smoke escaped his mouth as he spoke. "Did your brother show you how it works?"

"Yes."

"Open it."

I knelt and opened the case. The device itself—long and cylindrical, like a fat metal chair leg—was nestled inside like a snake's egg in a nest. The metal shell gleamed. The wires around it glistened. I drew it out and held it in my hands.

It was heavy, the metal cold against my skin.

"It does not call the Watchers to the house of the one who keeps it?" Atticus mused, his eyes on the device.

I started in surprise. "No..." I said. "It hasn't. Not once. And we've had it in our possession for weeks."

"I suppose that makes sense," Atticus mused. "The creatures guard the original gate in Echlos, do they not? They should not consider this one a threat, not if it is the same sort of technology as contained in Echlos."

I pondered this. Was this why we'd had no Watcher attacks on the house in the last few weeks?

"You know how to activate it?" he asked, interrupting my thoughts.

I nodded, and he watched with careful, precise attention as I unfolded the papers Jonn had given me, scanned the instructions again, and then pressed the raised swell of metal on one side of the device. My fingers trembled as light pulsed across the surface, and the wires sparked. I flinched. Atticus hissed in startled appreciation.

111

"Magnificent," he murmured. "A perfectly preserved piece of technology from that ancient age. It's marvelous. Your brother did well."

"Yes." I kept my eyes on the device as it spat blue fire from the tips of its metal tentacles and hummed a strange, high-pitched whine. A blue-green circle appeared above it, casting a perfectly symmetrical pool of light around us. My stomach churned. My heart pounded. Blood pumped through my arms and legs, and I was dizzy.

It was really working.

"Turn it off," Atticus commanded quietly. I hit the button, and the device's shrill squeal dropped to silence.

"I wanted to make sure you understood how to operate it," Atticus explained. "You will, of course, travel through the gate at Echlos like the rest of them."

I nodded and gulped a breath.

"Get your things," he said.

~

"You'll be fine," I said to my siblings for the hundredth time as I stood by the door, my cloak wrapped tight around my shoulders and a bundle of supplies in my arms. I had no idea what I'd need for this trip, so I'd scraped together another set of clothes and some food. "Ivy will handle all the quota delivery and attend the Farther school in exchange for food supplies as long as I'm gone. Everiss will handle the household and barn chores with Ivy's help, and do the cooking.

Jonn, you'll attend to the bulk of the quota, but Everiss can help you with that as you need her to. Ivy, Everiss—perhaps you could see to the traps—"

"I can do that," Ivy said. "I know where they are."

"All right. Ivy will check the traps."

They all watched me, wide-eyed, as I fumbled with my bag.

"I'll only be gone a few weeks. You'll be fine. Abel Brewer will help you if you need anything."

"What about Ann?" Ivy said. "Perhaps she—"

"Ann is in Astralux." Just saying the words made me feel sapped of all my strength.

Everiss's eyebrows shot up. "What?"

"What about Adam?" Ivy asked.

"He's gone, too."

They clearly wanted to ask more, but there was no time. Coldness seeped through me. Ann was gone. Adam was gone. I felt completely alone as I faced this difficult duty, but I would press on, because what other choice did I have?

I wanted to warn them about everything. I wanted to tell them about Atticus and how I didn't trust him, but they still didn't know about him, and I planned to keep them out of it entirely. No, I would complete this mission and return to them and everything would be fine.

"You'll be fine," I repeated, and they all nodded at me as if they were reassuring *me.*

"Go in safety, Lia," Jonn said. He grabbed my hand and squeezed hard. I hugged Ivy, and then, after a moment's hesitation, Everiss.

"Take care of them," I breathed into her hair, and she nodded and sniffled. Then I turned, sucked in a deep breath, and yanked open the door to the outside.

~

Echlos glittered strangely in the fading light of day. The sky was beginning to turn purple by the time we reached the shimmery net of deception that hid the ancient ruins from prying eyes. In the distance, the tops of the mountains scraped the sky.

I was the first one to step inside, breaking the seal of dark silence that filled the corridor below. Dust puffed and debris crackled and snapped beneath my boots as I moved forward down the tunnel of impossibly smooth stone. Behind me, I heard Atticus striking a match to light the lantern we'd brought.

"No," I called. "We don't need it. Save the fuel for your trip back."

He lifted an eyebrow questioningly, and I took another step forward. The ceiling glowed in response to my movement, and Atticus's jaw sagged.

Despite my anxiety, I grinned. Seeing him so astonished was strangely gratifying.

We descended into the bowels of the ruins slowly— down spiraling staircases tunneled into the depths, passing tarnished doors of gleaming metal and splashed stains of red and brown. Finally, we reached the massive room that housed the portal. My skin prickled in apprehension, and my scalp crawled. Our footsteps echoed as we entered the chamber.

"Incredible..." Atticus's voice whispered at the far reaches of the room.

The portal loomed against the far wall like a sleeping eye. I drew in a deep breath and crossed the room to the panel where Adam had activated it before. Jonn had explained how to do everything. I just had to find the switches.

Atticus followed. "Do you know what to do?"

"I know." I found the panel and tugged it open. Dust floated down from the edges. A cold wind swept through the hole in the roof high above us, ruffling my hair. I wrapped my fingers around the switch and yanked it down.

Nothing happened.

"Are you sure—" Atticus began.

Then, the air around us began to hum.

All the hairs on my arms rose. Light pulsed along the wall, tracing patterns in the gray. The circle began to gleam. The eye of the gate began to open. It unfurled slowly, like a mechanical flower spreading its petals to the sun.

Atticus stumbled back, his face glowing as he stared up.

"Magnificent!" he shouted.

Hot air rushed over us. I stared into the depths of the circle and saw only darkness. My heart plummeted to my feet, and my hands shook. I couldn't breathe.

115

Atticus grabbed my arm and tugged me around. "When you reach the other side, find a man called Jacob. He's from a place called Eos. That's how you'll know it's him. Give him this—give it to no one else." He put a sealed envelope in my hand. "It's the names of those we need. Keep your mission secret. And Weaver—" He raised both eyebrows at me. "Bring back only the ones on the list. Do not let emotional weakness compromise your mission."

Wait—a list? This wasn't part of the plan at all. *We're going to get them all back,* Adam had promised. All. Including Gabe.

Atticus saw my hesitation. "This is an important mission. You wouldn't want to compromise the safety of your family by failing."

A threat, I was sure of it. My eyes narrowed. But then, he was pushing me toward the gate. There was no time to think. "Hurry, there isn't much time!"

I shoved the envelope in my pocket beside the paper Jonn had given me.

This was it.

I clutched the bag of supplies tightly as memories of Gabe passing through the portal flooded my mind. I saw a young man, his expression determined as his eyes met mine for the last time, his mouth mashed closed as if to hold in a scream. I felt the rush of sadness and horror and hope that rushed over me as I watched him vanish behind the metal gates. My heart beat a rhythm against my ribcage as I stepped forward to the same place he'd stood. My pulse roared in my ears. The air crackled with an electric intensity, making all the hairs on my arms rise, and I could taste the power on my tongue. All I had to do now was step forward into that darkness. Jonn had explained it all as best as he understood from the journal. I'd fall, he had said, but gently.

All I had to do was close my eyes...and go.

I could hear Atticus behind me, muttering. I sucked in one deep breath, as if preparing to dive into a black lake from which there might be no return. My hands trembled. My stomach curled. My skin squeezed and my lungs expanded and my mind shrieked and the darkness closed around me and...

I fell.

ELEVEN

THE WORLD WAS gray as slate and icy as a river, and I was just a speck falling through the silence. Ribbons of cold air streamed through my fingers and wound around my neck. Pulses of sensation fluttered across my eyelids and cheeks and rushed over my arms. I was spiraling, spinning, soaring. Would this ever end? Time was long and short and I was lost in it.

All the air hissed from my lungs with a rush as I slammed into something hard and flat. Pain exploded across my skull and down my neck and spine. My teeth crashed together, and I felt a sputter of something hot gush down my cheek and hit my collarbone.

I lay still, stunned.

Gradually, I came back to consciousness. My head spun. Nausea swam over me in a sick green wave, and I heaved bile. I heard it splash as if from very far away. I tried to move, but my arms and legs weren't working. A whimper crawled up my throat, and then I was still again.

I cracked my eyelids open and tried to see. Everything was a white, amorphous blur. I fumbled for my sack, for the PLD. When my fingers found them, I relaxed and struggled to sit up, and gradually, my vision began to clear.

That was when I realized someone was reaching down to touch me. The outline of their body loomed like a giant above me.

I jerked back with a yelp and the person recoiled. I couldn't see the face, only the hands. They were large, meaty, with hair on the backs. A voice rumbled across my consciousness.

"Calm down, calm down—you don't want anyone to hear you, now." He made a sound in his throat. "Ah, you were sick on the floor. Well, don't move too much yet— you don't want to do it again."

I tried to stand and fell back. He muttered something and then said louder, "Here, here. Let me help you."

"Who are you?"

"I'm called Juniper," he said softly. "I manage to catch most of the fugitives coming across the divide, so you might say I'm the welcoming committee."

"Welcoming committee?" I mumbled. My head still spun, and the sound in my ears crackled. He tugged the sack from my limp hands, and I let him. I remembered the PLD hidden inside and I tried to protest. It came out as a weak mew, the sound a strangling kitten might make.

"Shhh." Strong hands hooked under my arms and hoisted me to my feet. My knees buckled, and I sagged against a warm chest that smelled like spice and forest. The round, cold shape of a button pressed into my hair.

I stumbled as I tried to take a step.

"Careful now," the man murmured. "You'll be fine. You're travelsick, but you're over the worst of it now."

Something hard touched my lips. The rim of a cup of some kind.

"Drink," he said.

I opened my mouth. Cold water trickled inside. It tasted so good against my parched tongue, and I guzzled greedily.

"That's it," Juniper said.

I squinted against the white light again, and this time the blurry shapes around me gained distinction. Walls stretched up far above me. Light lanced my eyeballs from an unknown, square-shaped source. I saw yellow barrels...a tangle of what looked like gray ropes...a strange, metallic fence. Faintly, I heard the sound of something chugging rhythmically. I smelled dust and the scent of old, secret things, like a cave.

"Where are we?" My throat rasped as I spoke.

"Let's just get you out of here," he said. "Then we'll talk."

Then, we were moving—he was half-dragging me as I stumbled forward on unsteady legs. We moved toward the blinding light, and I shut my eyes again and let him lead me. Cold air hissed through my hair, and we climbed a pair of steps. Warmth spilled over my head and across my arms. Sunshine. The wind hit my face.

It was hot.

"Quickly," Juniper urged. My feet hit packed earth, and I bumped against him. I cracked my eyelids open and tried to take stock of the landscape around me, but the light was too bright, too painful. I shut them again with a moan.

"It's the travelsick," he said soothingly. "You'll be fine in a minute or two."

His words spilled over me like little pebbles, bouncing off my awareness and tumbling away. I tried to listen, but the buzzing in my ears was fading in and out. Dimly, I heard the shrill cries of birds. Sweat broke across my back and between my shoulder blades. It was so hot here. Where were we?

Sudden shade enveloped us, and Juniper eased me down onto the ground. "Here," he said. "Lean back." My shoulders touched something hard and scratchy. Bark. A tree. I sighed.

He crouched in front of me. "Now," he said. "Try opening your eyes again."

I lifted my lids a fraction, then all the way. This time, the light didn't blind me. I gazed at the man. He was thick and burly, with a short brown beard and bushy eyebrows that hovered like caterpillars above his blue eyes.

"Better?" he asked.

I gulped and nodded. My head wasn't spinning anymore, and the roaring in my ears had faded. I looked around and saw that a sea of green enveloped us. Thick fir trees arched overhead, their branches waving in a faint breeze.

We were in a forest.

A dirt road led past us and around a bend. The way we'd come. I didn't see the place where I'd originally appeared, the cave-smelling place with the barrels and walls and fences. It was hidden by the trees.

"Where are we?" I asked. My voice was scratchy, as if long unused.

"The Compound," Jupiter said. "Along the southern side, near the workers' quarters."

"The Compound?" The name was meaningless to me. But it was so warm...we must be far south, or near the sea.

Adam's face filled my mind as I thought of the sea, because he'd lived at the coast once. My chest ached with hurt at the thought of him.

"What are you called, girl?" Juniper asked.

"Lia." I said it slowly, my gaze still on the surrounding landscape. My tongue tasted bitter and my mouth was chalky. I licked my lips and tried to swallow. "It's...it's so hot here."

"It's mid-spring," he said. "And we're going through a bit of a hot spell, too."

His voice faded in and out of my awareness as I gazed at something peeking from the edge of the trees. A long, white rail made of gleaming metal snaked past and disappeared around a corner, like a ribbon frozen in mid-flutter. It was beautiful and strange. Sunlight glittered along the edge and hurt my eyes.

"I'll let you rest a bit," Juniper said. "But we need to get inside. You can't stay here. They might see you."

"They?"

He didn't answer that.

A low rumble shook the ground. The air shivered. Pebbles skittered away from my feet and the leaves around us danced. I grabbed Juniper's hand. "What—?"

"It's just the transport," he said. "It won't hurt you."

Transport?

Something long and thin and large enough to be a string of wagons flashed from the trees, balanced atop that ribbon of gleaming metal. A flash of light and a blur of white and it was gone again. I drew in a fast breath. This was technology that I'd never seen the likes of before.

"It carries the workers through the Compound," he explained.

"So fast," I muttered.

"The Compound spans thousands of acres, all the way to the mountains." He waved a hand at the horizon, but the trees blocked my view.

"How does it move so fast?"

"It's powered by the sun," he explained.

When I was strong enough to stand, we made the laborious trip along the path through the forest. The trees didn't look so different from the ones in the Frost, except no snow coated these branches. A wind-swept sky the color of a robin's egg flashed in and out of sight through the waving tops of the trees. Birds shrieked overhead. Sunlight danced along the ground in dappled flashes. I felt sick, weary, and disoriented.

"I'll process you as soon as we get inside," Juniper was saying.

"Process," I repeated. My mind felt thick, my thoughts sticky. I was having difficulty thinking. "What do you mean?"

"We'll get you assigned a name, a job. We do it with all the travelers," he said. "The young ones are the hardest, but we find a place for them. We've been doing it for years."

"Are you a traveler, too?"

"One of the earliest," he said. His gruff tone signaled that he didn't want to talk about it.

"Is there someone here called Gabe?" I asked, and my voice came out strangled. My heart beat too fast with hope. I was lightheaded, dizzy. "He's a young man, thin, with light brown hair."

Juniper shook his head. "We got a couple young ones that fit that description, but I don't know that name. Everyone gets new names once they come." He paused. "Friend of yours?"

I jerked my head in an unsteady nod. My foot turned on a piece of gravel, and I almost fell. Juniper caught my elbow and hauled me back to my feet.

"You'll see everyone soon enough," he said. "We assemble weekly, and tonight's the night. You'll find your friend."

My stomach twisted with anxious anticipation.

We reached the edge of the forest and began to descend a hill. Unease prickled along my arms. Why did I feel so strange all of a sudden?

"There it is," Juniper grunted, pointing with his left hand.

I lifted my eyes, and my heart stuttered. I stared.

Ahead of me, utterly alien but at the same time recognizable even in its altered state, was a sight I'd see my entire life. The place I'd taken quota every week for years.

Iceliss. My village. The village where I grew up.

All the snow and ice was gone. The stones were fresh, unweathered by the elements. The Farther-built walls of metal and cages of steel were absent, and dozens of glittering buildings of a shimmering pale material clustered between the bones of the village that I knew, and yet...I could not deny what I saw. The shape of the hills cupped the town like two hands, cradling it. Overhead, a blue sky soared wide as a sail. The mountains reared up like sentries in the distance, topped with white. There was the path I'd walked my entire life, leading straight into the town. There were the streets, laid out in neat rows like lines drawn for a giant child's game of marbles. There was the hill that rose in the center of the village, and atop it, instead of the Mayor's house, a tall gray building with a curving roof stretched up like a questioning finger.

I turned to Juniper and found him watching my expression, his own bemused. "Some realize it faster than others," he said. "You're one of the fastest."

"I grew up here," I choked out. "This looks exactly like my village. The likeness is striking. Where are we?"

He barked a short laugh. "The better question, my girl, is *when?*"

TWELVE

"WHAT DO YOU mean, when?" I managed to stutter.

"The portal jumps back in time," he said. He spoke calmly, succinctly, as if he knew I wouldn't believe him and he wasn't particularly interested in convincing me. "You're at the same place you were before, just...about five hundred years in the past."

I wanted to vomit again. "How is such a thing possible?"

Juniper shrugged. "The portal allows it. The one from your time is special...different. It can bring travelers back, but the portals here cannot carry them the opposite way. Once here, they are stuck."

Unless they had the PLD, I realized.

My mind spun as I struggled to process this. I hadn't changed locations. I'd changed times. It was unimaginable. But...more unimaginable than a magic gate that transported its passengers? And I couldn't deny what I saw right in front of me. Iceliss. The village was the same, but completely different, too. The landscape was the Frost, but there was no snow. No ice.

No searing, brutal wind. Everything was bright and green and flowering. Everything was warm.

"Come on," Juniper said, handing me my bag back and gesturing for me to follow him. "I've got to get you to the others before anyone sees your odd clothes and asks too many questions."

We descended the path on the hill to the village. The streets appeared empty. Stone walls and houses I'd seen my entire life looked fresh and new, with none of the crumbling corners or weathered stains from centuries of snow and ice. Sunlight glittered on the surfaces of the strange buildings and sparkled on windowpanes. Everything was beautiful, graceful, like a garden of houses that had sprouted over the decay of the village I knew, and made it lovely. Vines crawled over walls and gates and waved in a faint breeze. Everything was beautiful, sparkling, and...empty.

"Where is everyone? Where are all the villagers?"

"The people who live here in the workers' quarters are mostly at the Labs during the day," Jupiter explained. "The scientists and other important people live on the other side of the Compound."

"Oh." Somewhere, I heard the chatter of voices speaking briskly, and the crunch of footsteps.

"This way," he said, tugging at my arm. We rounded a corner and plunged into a shaded alley. Relief seeped into me at the cessation of the sunlight.

"Why is it so hot here?"

Juniper spared me a glance. "This isn't so bad. Wait until summer."

Wait until summer. I wouldn't be here that long. He didn't know, of course. The PLD was heavy in my bag and the secret of it was heavy on my tongue, but I didn't mention it or my mission. I had to make sure I could trust him before I imparted that vital knowledge.

We reached a side street and turned the corner. Juniper escorted me past a row of bright yellow barrels and a stack of boxes. He stopped before a gray door set deep in the wall and produced a curious-looking sliver of metal from his pocket. He slid the piece into a slot, and I heard a low musical tone. He pushed it open and looked at me.

"Hurry," he said. "Let's get inside. Right now most of the workers are away at the Labs, like I said before, but they'll be back around dinnertime. I want you changed out of those clothes and out of sight before they return in case anyone sees you and asks questions. We'll work on your backstory while we wait for the others. There's a meeting tonight."

I wanted to demand immediate information about him, but my sense of self-preservation spurred me forward and made me shove the thought away for later. I stepped into the darkness of the doorway and he followed, shutting the door behind us. I clutched at my bag with both hands, feeling the comforting weight of the PLD inside. My heart thumped against my ribs. I heard another click, and light flooded the room, glowing from the ceiling as though it were made of moon dust. I scanned the space, taking stock of my surroundings, checking for danger. The room was small and plain. A desk and chair sat in one corner beside a curved window, and pale light slanted through the glass. On the opposite wall, shelves covered a wall from floor to ceiling.

"You can sit there," Juniper said, nodding at the chair. "Just stay quiet, and I'll bring you something new to wear. Are you hungry? Thirsty?"

"Thirsty," I said, my mouth aching for a drink as I sank into the chair and set my bag on my lap.

He jerked his chin in acknowledgement and disappeared through another door on the opposite wall. I heard another musical tone, and a strange whoosh. A breeze fanned my cheeks even though we were inside. The room was cold. I waited, shivering.

Juniper returned with a cup filled with an orange liquid. I sniffed it and then drank, too thirsty to care what it might be. It was ice-cold and tasted like sunshine. I drank it all.

"Feel better?" he grunted, studying my face carefully as he took the empty cup from my hand.

"Yes. Thank you." I looked around the room again. It was spare besides the shelves, table, and chair, giving me few clues about its purpose or the life of the person who used it. Was it Juniper's or someone else's?

I had so many questions. They began to flood over me, spilling from my tongue. "So the fugitives come in through a gate, and you find them and bring them here?"

He crossed his arms and paced to the window. Peering out it, he said, "Most times, yes. I clean the Jump Floor and the Deck, so I'm usually around the gate. I keep an eye out. And we have others who watch for anyone who shows up. So far, we've managed to escape detection, although we've had some close calls." He gave me a toothy grin. "You came during lunchtime. You're lucky."

Half of what he said made no sense at all to me, but I pushed on. "And the other fugitives...they're all still here?"

"Most," he said. "We've gotten them jobs around the Compound. Service duties, that sort of thing. Where else are they gonna go?"

"The Compound?" I asked. I wanted answers for all these unfamiliar terms I kept hearing.

"This," he said, waving his arms to mean the space. "Here. This whole place. This is where they keep the gate. They study the portals here."

"Scientists?" I guessed.

"Yes."

Adam had been right, I realized. But thoughts of Adam made my chest ache, so I pushed them away.

"It isn't cold here," I said. "In my time, it's cold most of the time."

"Yes," he said. "There've been a lot of changes between now and then." His expression turned curious. "Say, you're a lot more talkative than most. Most of the travelers who make the jump can barely string two sentences together."

"I was a little more prepared for this," I said simply, not wanting to talk about my mission.

That explanation seemed to satisfy him, and he nodded.

"You'll talk to Jake later," he said. "He's in charge of the fugitives who come here. Sort of the unofficial leader. He made the jump himself about three years ago—he was one of the very first ones to do it, and he did it all on his own. He's a smart one."

Jake. Could this man be the Jacob I was supposed to contact, the one I would give the list of names to? My heart beat faster, and sweat broke across my palms. "When can I see this man called Jake?"

"Tonight," Juniper said. "There's a meeting every week just to make sure everyone's doing all right, and it's tonight. You came at the perfect time."

He patted his hands on his vest and glanced around. "Well, I should probably see about getting you something else to wear. Come along, then."

We exited the door he'd gone through when he was fetching me the orange liquid. We stepped into a narrow hall, and I smelled must and rusty metal. The air was colder here.

"This is a food storage building," he explained. "So they keep it quite cold."

We descended a metal staircase into a cramped, shadowy room. Rows of narrow metal doors were mounted along one wall, and Juniper opened one and produced a wrinkled, dark olive piece of clothing all sewn together in one piece.

"Here," he said. "I think this will fit you. You can dress in there." He nodded at another doorway, and I saw a room of shiny white stone beyond. I took the clothing hesitantly. Boy's clothing, by the looks of it. I eyed the trouser-like legs and fumbled with the button-up front.

"Am I pretending to be a boy?"

"What?" He looked at me as if seeing my dress for the first time. "Oh, no. Most of the workers wear those here. Men and women."

Strange. I took the garment and went into the room he'd indicated. Shutting the door, I slid out of my dress. The olive clothing-piece felt tight and strange on my body, and I plucked at it nervously. I fingered my long blond braid and brushed at nonexistent dirt on my sleeve.

Suddenly, I was very afraid.

"We'll get you some food after this," Juniper called from the other room, making me jump. I shoved my dress into the bag I'd brought and hurried out again to join him.

~

The food he fed me was colorless but savory. I ate eagerly, ravenous despite the traumatic events of the day. My stomach hadn't been full in so long that I'd forgotten what it felt like. When I'd finished everything on the metal plate he'd offered me, I leaned back in the chair and sighed.

"We'll meet the others in an hour," Juniper said. He was working on something at the desk, although I couldn't see what it was. Musical sounds drifted from the desk and the tablet-like thing he held in his hands. "They'll be eager to hear your story."

My story. What would I tell them? My real mission was secret. I couldn't tell everyone. Only those whom it concerned. Atticus had strictly ordered as much. "I need to speak to the man named Jacob," I said. "I...I know someone who knows him." I stopped short of saying I had a message for him. It might arouse suspicion. Everyone else who came through the gate was running from something. If I showed up with a purpose, people might ask questions.

Juniper didn't notice my hesitation. "You'll meet him," he assured me, and returned to his work.

I shut my eyes and tried to sleep as the hours passed, because exhaustion plucked at my muscles and weighed down my bones. But my thoughts kept pinging between here and home. I thought of Jonn and Ivy. Were they frightened, overwhelmed? Would they be all right? I thought of Adam, of Ann. My eyes burned and I moved restlessly. I thought of Gabe, and a wave of nervous apprehension swept over me.

We hadn't seen each other in months. What would I say? What would he do? Did he still feel the way he'd felt before? These churning thoughts occupied me until Juniper shoved back his chair and stood.

"It's time," he said, and handed me a flat, metallic brooch inscribed with the words *Lila White*.

"What's this?"

"Your new identity," he said. "This means you're approved to be here. They'll get you a job in the kitchens or maybe on the swabber crew with me. Don't worry. You're going to be fine."

I took the piece numbly, and he helped me fix it to the front of my garment. When it was in place, he helped me up and led me back out into the gathering darkness.

The sun had almost set, and a blue-purple dusk had settled over the buildings and streets. The air was still warm, but no longer so hot it threatened to suffocate me. I breathed in deeply and smelled hints of snow blossoms and pine. Juniper motioned for me to follow, and we crossed the street and headed toward the outskirts of the town, which was near the tree line. I eyed the edge of the wilderness warily, conscious of the gathering darkness. "Are the Watchers very active lately?"

"What?" he asked. "Watchers?"

"The monsters," I said. "Whatever you call them here."

His forehead wrinkled, and then he nodded vigorously as if remembering what I meant. "Oh. Yes. I remember that word. Watchers. We don't have them here."

His words stunned me so much that I stopped walking. The legends said that the Watchers were ancient, as old as the Frost itself. Was it possible that they didn't exist in this younger, warmer land? A Frost without Watchers? I couldn't fathom it.

I didn't have time to ponder this new paradigm. Juniper was still walking, and I hurried to catch up. We reached the second building, and he motioned me inside first. "Straight down those stairs and to the right," he directed. He locked the door behind us, and I descended another metal staircase splattered with paint and grime. Faintly, I heard the murmur of voices. My stomach tied itself in a knot, and my hands turned clammy.

Would Gabe be here?

I stepped into a long, dimly lit room strung with pipes. A circle of individuals sat along the far wall, and the swell of their whispers reached me in a wave. They all glanced at me without really looking when I entered, and their mouths continued to move, but their eyes stayed fixed on me.

I scanned the faces. I didn't see Gabe.

A tall, thin man with dark hair and mismatched brown eyes stood and approached me. Juniper stepped to my side just as the man reached us. "This is Lila," he grunted. "Formerly Lia." To me, he said, "This is Jake. He's in charge of the fugitives."

"Pleased to meet you," Jake said. "I hope you've recovered from your jump."

Juniper patted me awkwardly on the arm and ambled off in the direction of the group. I supposed his work was done, and I wondered if I'd see him again. I felt a pang of nervousness. I'd felt safe with this gruff, short-spoken man. Who would be in charge of showing me around this strange place now?

The leader waited for my response. His expression was not unfriendly, but he was impossible to read. It reminded me a little of Adam, and sharp pang laced me.

"Yes," I said, trying to decide what to say to him. Should I mention Atticus now, or wait until I could be sure we wouldn't be overheard?

"Where do you hail from originally?" he asked. "Aeralis? The Southern countries?"

"The Frost," I said.

His eyebrows shot up, and his gaze sharpened almost imperceptibly. "Oh."

He looked like he might say more, but someone in the circle banged a cup against a pipe and called for everyone's attention. "Let's introduce you to the group," Jake said to me under his breath, and turned toward them.

Another man was speaking as we approached the circle. He stopped as we reached him, his gaze sliding to my face and then Jake's. He stepped back and shoved his arms across his chest. Clearly, the latter man was in charge.

"This is Lila," Jake said, waving a hand to indicate me. "She arrived today. Be sure to make her feel welcome."

As all eyes turned to me for the second time, I scanned the faces, looking for familiar ones. Where was Gabe? I didn't see him among the fugitives. Suddenly, my legs felt shaky and my stomach sick. Hands pulled me toward a seat, and I let them. The room spun. Was I getting travelsick again?

The man who'd been speaking stepped forward and resumed after I sank into the nearest empty chair. But his words ran over my head like water, and the whole room began to swirl and drip color as I struggled against the dizziness. Dimly, I heard the door open and shut as someone else entered the room. My vision darkened.

A hand grabbed my shoulder, anchoring me. A warm breath tickled my ear.

"Are you all right?"

I turned my head. My throat closed, and a pang sunk straight to my heart.

Gabe.

THIRTEEN

GABE'S EYES WIDENED and his face whitened as he saw me. "Lia." My name sounded strangled and strange coming from his lips, as if it were a language he'd almost forgotten how to speak.

I rose to my feet. We faced each other. We were inches and miles apart, our hands almost brushing, our breaths connected by an invisible thread stronger than steel. Were the others looking? I was aware of nothing but him.

"Let's get out of here," he managed, and then his fingers found mine, the heat of them branding me as he tugged me away from the others, and then we were passing through a door and into a dark hallway lit by a sputtering light that cast Gabe's eyes into shadow. He released my arm and stepped back. He lifted his hands to his face and then dropped them at his sides. "How...?" He made a noise in his throat. "I don't care," he said, and pulled me into his arms.

The hug startled me, and I stiffened. It had been so long since anyone had embraced me like this. But gradually, I relaxed against the warmth of him. His shape had grown unfamiliar in the past months, and I memorized the feel of him again.

"You're real," he muttered into my hair. "I can't believe it."

I blinked at the stupid tears that flooded my eyes as I tightened my arms around him, reassuring myself of the same thing.

He released me and stepped back. His eyes searched mine, looking for secrets. "Lia, how? Why?"

"I'm here on a mission for the Thorns."

"A mission? You—you work with the Thorns now? Those secret agents who helped me escape Aeralis? The group your parents belonged to?"

So much had happened since he'd left. It was too much to explain now. "Yes," I said, and choked on a laugh. "In a way, you inspired me to do it."

"But...now you're here," he said. "Your family. You—you left them?"

The secret of the PLD and my mission struggled on my tongue, rustling to life and demanding to be told. I sucked in a deep breath. I had to tell him, Atticus's orders be damned. "I didn't leave them," I said. "Not forever."

His eyebrows pinched together in confusion. His lips parted.

"There's a way to go back," I said. The words left me in a rush. I was empty after speaking them.

"What?"

"But it's a secret. Don't tell anyone. Not yet."

He nodded. His hands found my arms. "Tell me."

"I can't." The words burned the air between us. His gaze darkened, but I couldn't tell him. "Not yet—trust me, Gabe."

He nodded again. "Of course. I—I just can't believe it. When did you get here?"

"Today. Only hours ago. A man named Juniper found me."

"He finds most of us," Gabe said. "He's a little strange at times, but a good man. Trustworthy." He paused. "Have you gotten an ID card yet?"

I fumbled for the square with my new name and held it out. He studied it. "Lila," he read aloud, and then looked at me again.

Silence crept between us, broken only by the faint humming above our heads of some kind of machinery. My pulse still pounded in my ears. Nervous excitement still skittered across my skin. "So what happens now?" I asked.

"They'll find you a job," Gabe said. "Something to do. You'll learn to blend in, pretend you are from this time."

"How is it possible?" I asked. "How can we be here, in the Frost, in another time?"

"It's true," he promised.

The door opened behind us and a head peeked out. A red-haired girl, thin and freckled, looked at me curiously and then at Gabe. "Garrett," she said to him. "You coming back in? It's discussion time—didn't you have things you wanted to say?"

"No," he said. "Just tell them I went back to the rooms."

Her lips pinched, but she only nodded. She looked at me again, as if taking note of how closely we were standing to each other.

"Garrett?" I asked when she'd gone.

He shrugged. "We all get new names, *Lila*."

His tone was momentarily teasing, lighthearted. My mouth lifted slightly.

"Come on," he said after another moment. "I'll walk you to your room and show you around. Juniper hasn't done that yet, has he?"

I shook my head. "He hasn't."

"Come on, then." He seemed cheered by the prospect—it was something to do, something to keep us moving, keep us from having to struggle through the sudden awkwardness.

"I..." I hesitated. "I need to speak to Jake."

"He's already gone," Gabe said. "He left when I got here. He works in the Security Center, so he isn't here in the village much."

My stomach twisted. "When can I speak with him again?"

"Soon," Gabe said. "Don't worry. Let's go."

"My bag," I said, remembering.

We fetched my bag and then slipped out. The others were absorbed in their meeting, glancing our way but not lingering with their gazes. I was thankful. I didn't appreciate their scrutiny.

Our feet crunched against the gritty stone as we ascended the stairs. His hand brushed against mine, and sparks went up my arm, but we didn't clasp hands.

There was something in the air between us, a hesitancy born of months apart and a chasm of uncertainty brewing in my chest. I pushed the feeling away, because right now, how I felt was the least of my concerns. I needed to speak with Jake. Once I'd become certain that he was the Jacob Atticus had spoken about, I needed to deliver the sealed envelope to him and explain everything. And then...I had to wait for the next jump point. It would be almost two weeks, Jonn had explained.

The time seemed like an eternity to me now.

We reached the top of the stairs and stepped through a narrow door into the night. Stars glittered in a purple sky above our heads. We crossed a gravel-strewn street toward a line of low buildings huddled against the trees. The hot air enveloped me like a blanket, and I plucked at my sleeves as sweat prickled across my skin. "It's hot."

"The world is warmer here," Gabe murmured. "It isn't your Frost yet."

His hair had grown longer in the months since I'd seen him. Curls brushed the tops of his eyebrows and curled along the collar of his garments, which were olive-colored and all one piece like mine. His eyes kept finding mine and then darting away, as if he wasn't sure how to look at me, as if I were the sun, incapable of being gazed at.

Another question rose in my mind. "Juniper said there were no Watchers."

"It's true," Gabe said. He laughed, low and short. "The monsters are things of the future, too."

"Where do they come from?"

"I don't know."

We reached the buildings, and Gabe pressed his hand against the wall. The door slid open and we stepped into the cool darkness. Lights flickered on, illuminating another plain hallway. The air here chilled my skin and tickled my lungs.

"Technology makes the buildings cool," Gabe said. He led me down the hallway and stopped at an open door. "Here. This is yours."

I gazed inside. A small, square room with four white walls and a cot. A mirror, a window, a chair. It looked like a prison cell, and I said so.

"It's not much," Gabe agreed. "But it's safe."

"Isn't everything in this world safe?" I murmured. No cold, no Watchers...what could be frightening here?

A shadow flickered through Gabe's eyes and was gone. I might have imagined it, except for the words that followed. "Not quite."

Curiosity prickled me, but he didn't offer any more information.

I stepped into the room and set my sack by the cot. Gabe stood in the doorway, watching me with an unreadable expression. I faced him, expectant but not knowing what I was expecting. I felt exposed, a fish washed up on the bank, a turtle pried from its shell. My throat tightened. My hands brushed over the front of my strange garment.

Gabe opened his mouth to speak, but then we heard the clatter of footsteps in the hall. A pair of uniform-clad workers passed us. The moment turned awkward.

"I have so much to tell you," I began. Thoughts swirled in my mind—Korr, Atticus...Adam. There were so many things to say.

"Korr," I whispered finally. "He came looking for you."

Gabe's lips worked, but he didn't speak. He flinched at the name *Korr*.

"He's—he's in Iceliss. He's been torturing people, threatening people. Threatening me." Other memories assailed me...Korr letting me go, Korr talking about Gabe. *His brother.* "I know who he is," I said. "He looks just like you."

Gabe's eyelids flickered. "He's my older brother."

"I know."

He looked away, and a vein pulsed in his throat. He shifted against the door. "He's a terrible person."

"I know."

Gabe's lips flexed in a smile that quickly faded. "What is he doing in the Frost?"

"Looking for the device that brought me here...and looking for you."

He scowled. "For me?"

I nodded.

Gabe shoved his hands though his hair, pondering this, but he didn't comment on it. Instead he chewed his lip and asked, "When will we be able to go back to our own time?"

"Two weeks," I said. "That's when the next window of opportunity will be open, according to the journal my brother decoded."

More footsteps. Gabe looked over his shoulder and back at me. "I need to go," he said. "But we'll talk again soon."

"Soon," I promised, and then he was gone.

I took out the list Atticus had given me and opened it. I probably wasn't supposed to be looking at this, but I had to know if Gabe was coming back with us. Adam had assured me he was, but Adam wasn't in charge anymore.

My heart thudded with relief as I spotted his name. Gabriel. The only Gabe on the list. It had to be him.

I sank onto the bed in relief.

~

I woke abruptly, bathed in sweat. My consciousness clawed its way from the sleep that imprisoned me, and I sat up as I remembered.

The gate. The jump. The new world that was really just the old, only younger and hotter. Gabe. The PLD and my mission, hanging over my head like a freshly sharpened sword.

I threw back the blankets and reached for my clothes.

A sharp-faced woman with thick black hair and skin the color of amber stopped me in the hall. "You're the newest girl. Lila, right?" The square piece of metal dangling from her garment gave her name as Maida. Her hair bobbed when she spoke, and a thick silver cuff on her wrist made a clinking sound as she pointed at me.

I nodded. I wasn't sure of so many things in this strange world, so I supposed it would be better to keep my mouth shut and say as little as possible until I had a better sense of my bearings.

"You're late for breakfast," she said. "The commons building is that way." She pointed at the door with another jangle of her wrist, and I must have looked confused, for she sighed loudly. "You don't know where it is, do you?"

"No," I admitted, sticking to monosyllables.

She rubbed the space between her eyes with her thumb and forefinger. "Claire? Hey, Claire!"

Summoned by her named, a slender, red-haired girl emerged from one of the nearby rooms and sauntered toward us. I recognized her—she'd been in the secret meeting last night. She was one of the fugitives, the one who'd talked to Gabe.

If she recognized me, she gave no indication. Her face was a study in disinterest.

"Take Lila to the commons building and make sure she finds some breakfast," Maida said, and then she turned on her heel and disappeared down the hall.

I looked at Claire. She looked away. "Let's go," she said.

We didn't speak as we exited the building and crossed the gravel road together. Our feet crunched on the stones beneath our shoes. I tasted the hot, muggy air. Sweat prickled between my shoulders. I watched Claire carefully out of the corner of my eye. She walked easily, her arms swinging at her sides, her eyes scanning the streets as if she were looking for something or someone. She didn't look at me.

"So," she said eventually, with an air of studied casualness. "You're an old friend of Garrett's?"

She meant Gabe; it was his new name here. My scalp prickled. I glanced at her sideways. *An old friend?*

I wanted to laugh. In my mind's eye I saw Gabe crumpled in the snow, his blood seeping into his shirt and his hair wet with melting ice. I saw him huddled beneath a cover of straw in the barn, sweat prickling his upper lip and pain sharp and bright in his eyes. I saw him delirious with fever, screaming at the memories as he clutched my hand. I saw him standing, waiting to go through the gate, faith burning on his face and love on his lips.

"We were..." I began, and then stopped. I didn't know how to explain what we had been. We had not been betrothed. We had not been courting. We had not been declared as anything, and I didn't know how he felt now. He had loved me once, I believed that, but love was like a vine. It could wind into the cracks of your heart and bind you to another like chains, or if left untended, it could wither at the roots into something cold and lifeless and brittle.

I hadn't seen Gabe in months. He'd felt passion before, but I didn't know how he felt now. How could I fight for something if I was so uncertain about it? And what about Adam? My chest ached like a bruise just thinking his name.

"We were friends," I agreed.

Claire grunted, acknowledging my answer.

Silence blanketed us as we crossed the road and reached a cluster of simple stone buildings huddled against the trees. The town.

I was struck anew at how clean and unscarred everything looked. The familiar bones of stone were there—walls, streets, buildings—but they all gleamed fresh in the early morning sunlight, like a collection of newly crafted pots straight from the kiln, with no lichen or stains to mar their surfaces. No cracks or fissures birthed from years of suffering in wind and cold laced the walls or veined the streets. New bronzed metal sparkled on doors, windows, steps. A veneer of glitter seemed to infuse everything, like magic. This younger age wore its technology like gaudy jewelry. Sounds of machinery hummed faintly in the distance. Birdcalls mingled with the grind of gears. Somewhere, I heard a burst of tinkling music, and then a glass door slid open and a stream of robe-clad young men and women emerged, laughing. They headed for the path into the forest.

"Students," Claire said. "They are here to study the gate, and the technology it uses."

Walking through the buildings seemed like a dream. I recognized the quota yard only from its position. Strange vehicles filled it, glittering in the sunlight. A man dressed in a flowing blue garment walked between them. He didn't look at us. We moved on.

We passed what would one day become the Meeting Hall in my village. The elaborate carvings were missing, as well as the wooden doors painted blue. Instead, I saw plain walls of shimmering glass material and an elegant, curving roof. Ivy grew wild and dripped over the sides.

"That's the library," Claire said, seeing me looking at it.

A gold-colored vehicle with panels like furled wings swished past us, horseless and swift as wind. I backed up fast, the backs of my heels hitting the wall behind me. Claire's eyes darted to mine.

"Don't be afraid," she said, but I could tell she thought her words would make no difference. I could tell she expected me to cower anyway.

I wouldn't do it. I was a Weaver. I walked the Frost at night. I smuggled fugitives from the frozen forests to the gate in Echlos. I had looked Watchers in the face and not died. I had kept my family from starvation.

I lifted my chin and stepped forward again without hesitation. Surprise crossed her face, and then she smiled a little. She followed me toward our destination.

But before we reached the buildings, Claire reached out and snagged my arm. I stopped and looked at her, ready for anything. My heart stuttered. Would she threaten me, make me her enemy, stake a claim on Gabe's affections?

But her gaze was not unfriendly. "About my comment before," she said, biting her lip. "Garrett and I are friends," she said. "But nothing more. If he is your young man—"

"He isn't spoken for," I said, speaking hastily, almost sharply. "I...he isn't mine."

"I understand. I just didn't want you to think anything of my question."

I nodded once and we dropped it. The silence felt easier after that, and her shoulders were less rigid as she walked beside me.

We reached the door of the first building in the cluster, and she opened it. We stepped inside into a cloud of cool air and scents of breakfast. As the smell of food hit me, my mouth watered and my stomach pinched with sudden, violent hunger. I hadn't eaten since the afternoon before, and now my legs shook.

I'd been hungry for so long.

The room was filled with sunlight. Windows sparkled along the walls and ceiling. Tables and chairs of metal filled the center floor. Mounds of steaming meats and breads filled a row of tubs along one wall. It was a feast, a veritable mound of food. I hadn't seen such excess except in my dreams. I reached out a hand to steady myself against the wall as excitement raced down my arms and whipped my stomach into a riot of nervous delight.

"Try not to eat too much," Claire advised from her place beside me. "We're all hungry when we come, but this food is rich. They aren't accustomed to hunger here."

We piled plates high with food and sat at a metal table by the windows. I closed my eyes as I took the first bite of something that was shaped in cubes but tasted like sausage. The flavor exploded on my tongue, and I sighed.

When I opened them, Claire was watching me again.

"Did you know Garrett in Astralux?" she asked.

I wondered—had he told her anything of his past? I blinked, not knowing how to answer. Instead, I took another bite, and she must have interpreted my silence as reticence to talk about my origins.

"I'm sorry," she said. "I didn't mean to pry. We aren't supposed to ask unless the other person brings it up first. It's one of our biggest rules."

"I'm just surprised he speaks about his past," I said finally.

"He doesn't," she said. "He never says a word. I only know he's from Astralux because I saw him there."

My interest sharpened. I put down the fork and leaned forward. "Saw him there? You mean...before he was a fugitive?"

"Yes. Of course. At functions at the palace. My father was a tailor and I sometimes attended functions. We never spoke, of course."

My heart crashed against the walls of my chest, and my pulse thundered. "Palace?"

"Yes," Claire said, and her eyes widened slightly with surprise as she realized I was startled by this information. "He's a prince, a member of the royal family."

151

Prince? Royal family? As in the royal *Aeralian* family?

Suddenly, I couldn't breathe.

FOURTEEN

I STARED AT her across the table, open-mouthed. Gabe was an Aerialian prince?

"You're wrong," I said, even though pieces were clicking into place and shivers were beginning to cascade down my spine. Gabe's clear good breeding and signs of obvious wealth. All the Farther soldiers who'd braved the dangers of the Frost searching for a single, frightened fugitive when they'd never done such a thing before—clearly, he must be an important prisoner to warrant so many soldiers. I recalled his noble habits, his vocabulary, his gestures, and the aura of grave importance that clung to him like a lingering scent.

And then there was Korr. He was a nobleman, a person of wealth and position. A man of influence...and he was Gabe's brother. I remembered the way Raine had deferred to him, almost feared him.

A bird landed behind the window and peered at us with bright black eyes. It fluttered its wings and hopped on the ground, looking for crumbs, and I gazed at it while shards of the truth sank into my soul. "You're wrong. You must be wrong," I repeated, but my words were dull and lacked inflection.

Claire's eyes softened as if she understood something. As if she'd just solved a puzzle. I didn't like being a puzzle that she was solving. I bristled.

"Whatever you say," she murmured, and then turned her head to look out the window as if suddenly fascinated by the bird.

I struggled to draw in a deep breath. I glanced down at my food, which had begun to congeal on my plate. I was no longer interested in eating it, despite my hunger. My mind churned with a cacophony of memories, thoughts, and denials.

How could this be true? How could he have hidden it from me?

Claire fiddled with her spoon and bit her lip. Finally, she broke the silence. "Well," she said, shooting me a quick glance. "We should get going. I have to take you to the work site before I can report to work myself. I don't want to be late."

Despite my sudden lack of appetite, I shoveled the last few bites of food into my mouth before pushing my plate away. Even extreme shock wouldn't keep me from eating. Months of near-starvation tended to put things into perspective. Claire waited, tapping her fingernails against the table.

After I'd finished eating, we put our plates in a hole in the wall meant for dirty dishes, and then we exited the building. The hot air struck my face and sucked the breath from my lungs. I followed Claire up the street. I recognized the shape of what would become the artisans' quarter in my village. To my left, I saw the place that would become the markets. At the moment, it was only an empty square filled with barrels.

Claire stopped before a curving metal door just beyond the market space. "You'll receive your work assignment here. Good luck."

I jerked my head in a nod, and she left me standing there alone. I took a deep breath and entered the building.

The room was small and lined with shelves just like Juniper's room had been. Bright light glowing from the ceiling hurt my eyes, and a humming sound buzzed in the distance like the whining of an insect. The scent of dust and soap filled the air, a contradicting promise of unwashed corners and cleaned surfaces. A spider crawled along the edge of the ceiling, near the light.

A woman sat at a table a few paces away, gazing down at a stack of papers. When I entered, she looked up and frowned, as if she'd just been presented with a particularly unpleasant problem to solve. Her eyes crinkled at the corners as she squinted at me, as if she was trying to place my face in her memory. "You're the newest girl?"

I nodded.

"Funny," she said. "Your face is familiar. I wonder..." her voice trailed off, and she raised an eyebrow.

Sweat broke out between my shoulder blades. Did she suspect something? Was something about my face, my mannerisms, my clothing suspicious? My stomach curled in apprehension as words hovered on her lips, unspoken.

She licked her teeth. "Hmm," she said.

"I arrived yesterday." My lips felt stiff. What if I gave her a wrong answer? What if my accent, my words gave me away? My fingers dug into my palms as I waited for her to make another comment.

But after an excruciating few seconds, she flicked her hand as if waving away a cobweb. "Never mind," she said, and reached across the desk for a stack of papers. "This has your information. There's a need for another member of the cleaning crew in the Labs. You'll have to be cleared with security first. You can do that there." She pointed at a doorway in the far wall and then looked away.

Clearly, I was dismissed.

My legs wobbled and my stomach lurched as I headed for the door, clutching the paper. I'd escaped one potential trap, but now I was faced with another. What were they going to do? Would I have to pass a test?

I stepped into another hallway, another room. More bright lights, more endless rows of shelves. More scents of dust and soap. But fortunately, I wasn't asked any questions this time. A man in a white coat marked my fingers with ink and pressed it onto a warm square that blinked and beeped. He shone a bright, focused beam into my eyes and then checked a thin tablet in his hand. He grunted an affirmative sound. "Lila White."

I expected him to ask me questions, but he only turned away.

My breath escaped my lungs in a hiss. I was running blind here. I had no knowledge of this place, no knowledge of what to say. Irritation surged in me. Why hadn't anyone given me instructions yet? I needed more knowledge if I was to complete this mission unscathed and undetected. What would they do if they discovered I was an imposter? Evict me from this place? Imprison me?

But when the man turned back, he only handed me square of metal that clipped to my garment. He didn't ask any more questions. "This shows that you're allowed in the Labs," he said. "You'll need it at all times in the Labs, so don't lose it."

"I won't."

"You ought to report right away," the man added. "They'll be expecting you with the other swabbers. Do you know how to find the Labs?"

"I..."

"Oh, I'll take her."

I went still at the familiar voice. *Gabe.* I lifted my eyes and saw him standing in the doorway, his head tilted so his hair fell over his eyes and his left shoulder braced against the doorframe casually. He carried a box under one arm. "I'm going that way."

"Are those the tests I'm expecting?" the man asked, and Gabe nodded.

My skin prickled and my mind spiraled as I watched him set the box on a low table. He turned and looked at me, his face impassive.

"Ready?"

"Yes."

He swept an arm to indicate that I pass through the door before him. The gesture was grand, almost stately. Claire's words flashed across my mind.

I know he's from Astralux because I saw him there. He's a member of the royal family.

Little explosions of pain danced in my chest.

Our eyes met and our clothing brushed as I passed him to step through the doorway. His were deep, unfathomable. His eyebrows lifted at what he saw in mine. I could only imagine what daggers I might be shooting at him. A confusion of feelings crawled at the back of my mind, a cacophony of thoughts fighting for dominance. I went out into the bright, oppressive heat and waited for him to catch up while the feelings cascaded over me in a wave of images. I remembered the shirt I'd torn from his back the first day I'd found him— the feel of fabric fine and silken against my fingers, fabric that was completely useless in the cold but that spoke of wealth, opulence. I remembered the story he'd told me, about his sister's birthday, about how the soldiers took him from the house. I remembered him choking on astonishment when I asked about his family's occupation, and the way his face had sobered as he'd searched for something to say.

Gabe reached my side. I wanted to speak, but when I looked at him, the words in my throat refused to come out. He shoved his hands in his pockets and nodded at the trees. "The Labs are this way. Shall we walk?"

I let him lead me up the path. The sunlight shone against his hair and turned the edges golden. I stared at his back. Finally, I found the words. They came out suddenly, shattering the stillness. "Why didn't you tell me?"

Gabe stopped. His shoulders and neck stiffened. "Tell you what?" His tone was cautious.

My fingernails dug into the palms of my hands as I spoke again. The words felt like vomit coming up my throat. "That you are a member of...of the Aerialian royal family. A prince."

He flinched and turned, and I read the sharp refusal in his eyes, but I also saw the fear. He was begging and defying me at once without speaking. At his sides, his hands clenched just like mine. For a single shimmering moment, tension hung between us. Birdcalls snapped the silence. The heat clung to my skin and made me sweat. There were so many things to say. I didn't know where to start. I didn't know how.

"It's not—" he began, and stopped. He sighed. "I was a prince. Before the soldiers overthrew everything. Before the coupe. Now, I'm just a beggar with fine manners. Worse, I'm a fugitive hiding for my life."

"What else haven't you told me?"

He just shook his head.

Everything we'd shared, everything we'd risked, everything we'd given, yet he'd held this back. The truth of it made me feel old, dried up, empty. Keeping such secrets left me vulnerable. It put me at risk. But more than that...it was Gabe. I thought we trusted each other.

"Why didn't you tell me such a momentous thing?" I demanded, and this time my voice crackled, giving me away.

Heat rose in his face and settled behind his eyes, flickering like defiance. "It was too dangerous. I didn't know if I could trust you. And I...I still don't." His throat bobbed as he swallowed.

That admission cut me like a knife, sensible as it may be. Anger spiked in me, hot and furious. "I risked my life for you. I risked my family's lives for you! I cared for you when you were sick and braved the Watchers in the forest to see you to safety. I..." I faltered before saying those three fatal words. *I loved you.*

"But..." His eyes pleaded with me to understand. "My political identity is my biggest secret. My greatest vulnerability. I don't dare trust anyone with it. Anyone who knows might use it against me, or against my family."

Footsteps rang out, and a string of workers in gray garments emerged from the trees, following the gravel path toward the village behind us. Gabe and I fell silent, waiting until they had passed. His chest rose and fell with tight breaths. His eyes were too bright, like flames. "Listen," he said, as soon as they'd gone. "Please. We'll talk about this later. You have to understand, Lia. I just...couldn't."

I nodded. I couldn't speak.

We resumed walking, side by side but miles apart.

The path wound through the forest. Trees crowded both sides of the path, striping us with shadows and sprinkling speckled patches of sunlight at our feet. The air here was cool and heavily scented with pine. I scanned the landscape for landmarks to tell me where we were, but I recognized little here in the woods. I saw only trees and hills. Not the sort of things that would look the same after five hundred years.

But when we rounded the final curve, I inhaled sharply. A faint shimmer filled the air, like the inkling of a dream, and then we were through it. Ahead, at the top of the hill, a cluster of rounded roofs made from shimmering white material shot up abruptly from the trees. Behind them I saw the mountains framed by a sweeping blue sky.

It was *Echlos.*

FIFTEEN

"ECHLOS," I BREATHED.

Gabe stopped and swung to look at me. He seemed surprised that I hadn't known. "Yes," he said. "Here, they call this place the Labs. Echlos is the name of the organization who built it, but it is the same place where they keep the gates, the place you took me that night."

Dazed, I stared at the sight before me. The structure looked so different beneath this warm blue sky, free from snow or debris or crumbling vines. New, clean, sparkling. Beautiful. Part of the river had been diverted to flow across the front of the building, and it fell in a ribbon of silver between two bridges that led to the doors. All around us, ferns and rushes shivered in the breeze.

"Come on," Gabe said, reaching out for my arm, but he stopped before he touched me and let his hand fall. He stepped forward toward the buildings, and I followed him along the paved white path that snaked up the hill, a path that would crumble away in the 500 years between my time and this one. My stomach fell as we reached the shadow of the doors, a place that was now just a hole in my own time. They gleamed silver in the sunlight.

They swished open with a musical tone, and the wind blew my hair back. I resisted the urge to gasp. We stepped inside, and again I was struck by how familiar and yet how strange it all was. The hallway I recognized from before stretched ahead of us, but now it was free from dust and grime. The floors shone. The ceiling burned bright as a captured sun. The air smelled faintly of something sharp and metallic.

We descended a flight of steps, the same flight of steps I'd descended with Adam only months previous. On the wall, I saw the painted letters. ECHLOS. I breathed out. I reached up and touched them lightly with my fingertips. Shivers crawled over my skin, and I knew if I shut my eyes, I'd see the memory of the dimly lit cavern and Adam's dark eyes meeting mine.

"Come on," Gabe said softly, jogging me back to the present. We continued to the bottom of the stairs and down a long hall.

"Garrett?"

We both turned at the voice that had called Gabe's other name. A thin man in a white robe stood at the end of the hall, eyeing us curiously. He had silver-white hair that brushed the edges of his shoulders and a long, narrow chin. When he frowned at us, his mouth puckered.

"Hello, Doctor Borde," Gabe said. His tone was respectful, cautious.

A shiver went through me from my scalp to my toes. *Doctor Borde.* The man Jonn had asked me to get a piece of paper to.

"Do you have those deliveries I've been expecting?" the man asked. "I've been waiting for half an hour."

"Yes, sir." Gabe produced a sheaf of papers and passed them to the man. The doctor took them and examined them briefly before raising his head to regard me.

"Who is this?" he asked.

"Lila," Gabe said, after the slightest hesitation as he remembered my new name. "She's the newest swabber for the Labs."

Borde's gaze slid over me, and I felt as though he were examining every freckle of my face. His blue eyes burned like lightning in his wrinkled face, and his white hair quivered as he tipped his head to one side. "Lila," he repeated, as if committing it to memory. "You...remind me of someone."

I didn't know what to say, so I didn't say anything.

After another moment, he nodded and disappeared down the hall.

"That was odd," Gabe said, releasing his breath in a sigh. "We aren't supposed to attract too much attention from the stationaries."

"Stationaries?"

"People who haven't jumped. People who belong in this time."

"Oh. And who was that?" My heart thumped as I tried to keep my voice even.

"Doctor Borde...he's one of the head scientists here. Not exactly someone we want scrutinizing us. But he's an odd one, so perhaps it doesn't matter too much—now come on."

I wanted to ask more questions, but I didn't want to signal that I was overly interested in Borde. I didn't want anyone to know about Jonn's little side mission that he'd given me.

We passed more gleaming doors and descending another set of stone stairs that curled in an endless spiral. My heart pounded at the glitter and bustle around us. "Tell me more about this place."

"What do you want to know?"

"Everything."

He laughed in a way that indicated I'd better pick a topic, because there was too much to even begin to sum it all up without direction. I searched my mind for what I wanted to say. I thought of the woods we'd passed through to get here, how we'd traveled without fear. "There are no Watchers?" I asked finally.

"No," he said. "And no Frost."

"Why is it so warm? Where is the snow?"

"The coldness hasn't begun, and won't for another century," he said. "It happens after."

"After what?"

"I don't know," he said. "Whatever happens that makes all...all *this* go away." He waved his arms to indicate the shining halls and gleaming floors, and in my mind's eye I saw the withered hallways of crumbled stone that they would one day become. "Whatever happens to end it," Gabe said. "Obviously, it'll be something big. This place is largely untouched in our

165

time. The gates remain, and the buildings...but the people all left."

That made my chest ache strangely. I ran my tongue over my lips, thinking. I remembered something he'd said to Borde. "What's a swabber?"

Gabe snorted. "That's what they call the people who clean the floors and decks around here."

"So I'm a swabber?"

He jerked his head in a nod. "Swabbers are mostly seen and not heard, so try not to talk to anyone."

I imagined I would have little difficulty following that advice.

Gabe continued down the hall, and I followed. Our footsteps rang hollowly as we turned the corner. Cool air rushed over us. I sucked in a sharp breath.

The room arched up and away into a vast space, just as I remembered. Gone was the hole in the roof that let in snow and sunlight. Instead, a smooth arch of pristine white glowed with inner fire. Gone were all the stains and debris on the walls. In their place, colored markings of paint—lines, numbers—made neat, orderly rows, and snaking cables curved along the walls like coils of gray intestines. We were in the bowels of Echlos here. A smooth, clean floor of stone stretched ahead of us, and at the end of it, I saw *it*.

The gate.

The circular metal frame of the portal glittered beneath the glow of the lights. Blue fire flickered in the seams, and a hum electrified the air and made my hair stand on end. It was alive today, seething with power and energy. A flicker of corresponding excitement curled in my stomach, responding to the tug of energy that swirled around us. I stared at it, transfixed. This was the gate that had brought me here.

But it could not take us home. We needed the PLD for that.

Red lights flashed above the gate, and slowly I became aware of the figures dressed in gray garments who roamed at the base of the portal, checking things and pausing to speak to one another. They wore goggles and masks that obscured their faces and made them look strange, alien.

"How do the jumpers arrive without being seen?" I asked Gabe in a low voice. "Won't these people see them?"

"We've worked out a system," he said. "We have fugitives working everywhere here, watching things. So when the gate begins to power up, we pull a switch that clears the floor. It's a random emergency test that happens regularly and without warning. Everyone clears out, and we can take the new arrival to safety."

Simple and elegant. I nodded, impressed. "How many come through?"

"Not many. I was one of the last," he said. "Except for two children, and now you."

I remembered those two children, lost and frightened and bruised, shivering in the woods when I'd discovered them. "What happened to them?"

A smile flickered across his face, a brief quirk of his lips that made my stomach twist at the familiarity of it.

"They are thriving. They learn at the school and play in the town. They're too young to work, so we said they were the children of one of the fugitives. They are happy. They don't talk much, but they smile. And they aren't so skinny anymore."

A rush of warmth and affection pooled in my chest at the thought of those frightened children being safe and whole now, and I smiled at him in relief. Gabe's eyes widened slightly, as if he couldn't believe that I was looking at him with such warmth. He stared at me thoughtfully for a moment before allowing his mouth to curve slightly in response.

For a brief second, I was transported to another time, another place. We were surrounded by cold air and swirls of snow, and his heart was bleeding into mine as we whispered words to each other in front of my farmhouse.

But I blinked, and the memory was gone. The hum of the gate behind us pulled my thoughts from him to the present. The chafe of my garment and the heat of the surrounding air reminded me that I was here. I needed to focus. I needed to complete my mission.

There wasn't much time.

"I need to speak to a man called Jacob," I said. "I have a message to deliver to him. I think it's Jake. Can you get me to him?"

"Jake works at the Security Center," Gabe explained. "You already have a pass to be at the Labs. Jake mentioned to me that they have a job for a swabber open at the Security Center. That way you'll have regular access to him if you have any questions—he's almost always working."

I nodded. "Perfect. How do we do that?"

"I'll arrange it," he said. "For now, let me show you your duties here."

He showed me the cleverly hidden closet and the bronzed door that hissed open from its hiding place in the wall. And for all the technology of this world, the cleaning devices were simple mops and brooms. I almost snickered.

A few other swabbers moved around us, retrieving things from the closet and eyeing me with undisguised curiosity. True to what Gabe had said about being seen and not heard, they all stayed silent. They wore garments identical to mine, and most of them looked weary. I noticed Claire among the others, but she did not acknowledge either of us. Her red hair bobbed as she bent to grab a mop, and then she turned and headed down the hall.

A faint frown creased Gabe's mouth, but he said nothing. He didn't look her direction, so I didn't, either.

When Gabe had finished explaining the cleaning duties, he handed me a mop and pointed me toward one of the hallways, then he left to arrange the final things for my job at the Security Center.

The other swabbers avoided me. They didn't speak or make any noise except an occasional whistle. Sharp and short, low and long—the calls varied, and soon I realized they were a sort of communication. I listened, trying to detect patterns. I saw Claire again as she passed me in the hallway, but we didn't look at each other. She put her mop away and vanished around a corner.

I mopped floors until my arms ached and I could see my reflection shining back at me in the tiles. With all their technology, couldn't they find some other way to clean these floors? As I worked, my thoughts wandered between the problems facing me. I needed to find Jacob and deliver the message from Atticus. That was my most pressing concern. And I needed to figure out a way to give Jonn's message to Doctor Borde. But...my mind kept returning to the Frost. That world seemed so impossibly far away now—the snow, the dark forests, the gray-uniformed soldiers, the creatures in the night. My heart ached when I thought about those who were there. Jonn. Ivy. Were they all right? Was Everiss helping them? And Ann...Adam. They were gone without me. It should be Adam here now, finding Jacob and delivering the message and getting the fugitives we needed back to the Frost. He was the one who would have known what to do. Instead, it was me. Adam had insisted I take the job instead, Atticus had said.

And I'd never felt so lost and helpless.

But I gathered resolve around me like the folds of a cloak. I could do this. I had no choice but to do it, and I would succeed. Because anything else was not an option.

One of the swabbers whistled a short, piercing note, and they all melted away. I stopped, confused.

The clip of footsteps along the halls made me pause. A dark-haired man with narrow, sharp eyes and wearing the flowing robes of a scientist rounded the corner. He stopped when he saw me, and my heart wrenched abruptly when our gazes met.

He reminded me of Adam, and I flinched as I remembered that Adam had left without telling me, leaving me to this mission alone.

"Excuse me," the man said coldly, noticing the wet ground at his feet. "I'll go another way." And then he frowned at the route he'd just come, as if unable to calculate how he was going to accomplish this. Lines appeared across his forehead, and he turned and contemplating the path where I'd just mopped.

I only wanted to avoid any long conversations or scrutiny. I didn't need anyone asking me too many probing questions. I simply wanted him to move on.

"Just go across carefully," I said. "Don't slip."

He nodded and spared me a brief smile before venturing across the wet tiles. He stepped gingerly, and his mouth worked with concentration.

Another scientist appeared at the end of the hall.

"Doctor Gordon," he called, and the dark-haired man lifted his head to reply to the other scientist. His feet wobbled on the slick floor, and he grabbed the wall to avoid falling. Hissing a curse, he darted a dirty look my way and moved forward to greet the one who'd called out to him. "Swabbers," I heard him mutter. "Always underfoot."

A few of the others appeared, and all of them eyed me warily. I grimaced. So much for staying out of the way. I'd managed to attract more than enough attention for one day. I saw Claire looking at me, and I returned her stare until she turned away. Satisfaction swirled in my chest—a small victory, but one nonetheless.

More footsteps sounded, and again the swabbers seemed to melt away. This time, Gabe appeared. "I secured your pass to the Security Center," he said. No mincing of words, not between us now. He looked around, noticing that I was alone, and then he shrugged. "Let's go."

I swallowed to ease the dryness in my throat. I put away the mop with shaking hands and then followed him up the spiraling staircase.

~

The sky had begun to turn dark when we finally emerged into the open air. Purple shadows lined the paths and crept from the trees. A smattering of stars sprinkled the sky, and in the distance the moon was just a sliver of faint white.

"This way," Gabe said, and we took one of the paths into the forest again. Some of the paths were elevated, I noticed, held aloft by gleaming white struts. Vehicles zipped past on them, moving at impossible speeds. The wind from their passing stirred my hair. Soft glowing strips of light lit the paths and illuminated our steps. Around us, the chirps of animals filled the air.

"Are you in charge of my assimilation?" I asked Gabe after a moment of silence. "I thought Claire...?"

He flinched slightly at the mention of her. "I asked to be assigned to you." His tone was careful, guarded. Not quite apologetic. Defensive, maybe. "I need to talk to you. Explain things better."

"There isn't anything to explain." I feel hollow saying it. Foolish. I was the practical one. Why couldn't I accept this? "You didn't trust me. I understand."

A sigh escaped him, and he scrubbed both hands through his hair in a display of sudden frustration. His mouth opened and closed, and his fingers clenched into fists. "My family was in great danger," he said. "We were being watched all the time. The political coup had happened bloodlessly. My uncle died of natural causes, and instead of the rule passing on to my cousin, the soldiers stepped in and the dictator took over. He moved us from the palace. He put us under guard. We were treated well, only put under house arrest. We were paraded about as if we were all friends, as if we approved of his rule. He even began courting my sister." His voice thickened in disgust and he paused for a moment and looked around at the trees. The sky above us glittered with starlight. "It's dark there," he said finally, in a wistful tone. "The city of Astralux is cold and wet from the swamps that surround it. The sky is filled with steam and machinery and metal." He sounded wistful now. "So different from the Frost...all that blinding white and blue sky and trees. So different from here."

My lungs felt tight as I listened. In my mind's eye I saw him, trapped in the Aeralian capital of Astralux, the city ironically called light when it was surrounded by darkness and fog. I saw the lights glowing in the perpetual mists that clothed the city from the swamps. I heard the mechanical clocks ticking and the airships whirring overhead and the stamp of soldiers' boots, and I shivered as a sick feeling crawled over me. A feeling akin to helplessness and panic. I sucked in a deep breath to calm myself.

Gabe clasped and unclasped his hands. "I wouldn't let that bastard marry my sister to solidify his position. He was a monster. So when revolutionaries approached me—"

"The Thorns?" I asked. My skin tingled.

He shook his head. "I don't know. I first heard from a member of the old Senate, which had since been turned into a sham. He was not the instigator, simply a messenger. I agreed to help. I agreed to take part. And when the soldiers came for me..." he trailed off and stared into the distance a moment. "They knew what we'd been planning. They knew about me. Someone told them. Someone I trusted."

The word *who* burned on my lips, but I wouldn't speak it.

"So I couldn't tell you," he said. His eyes finally dragged up to meet mine, and I read the pain and confusion there. "I couldn't tell anyone. I'd been betrayed. I had no one left who was safe."

"I understand," I said, and this time I truly did.

We resumed walking in silence.

174

"And now my brother, Korr, works with the enemy," Gabe spat. "According to what you've told me. It doesn't surprise me. He was always a sympathizer. Even when we were children, he couldn't be trusted for anything. And when the dictator came to power, Korr was the first one to lick his boots in submission."

I thought of the dark-haired, smirking Korr, and *submission* was not a word that came to mind. Instead, I saw someone willing to do anything he had to do to get what he wanted. Perhaps that was even more dangerous.

The path curved abruptly and revealed a long, low building nestled among the trees. Beyond it stretched a circular clearing of grass and stones. The gray walls and dark roof of the building blended with the shadows, and the low lights that lit it twinkled like tiny stars. Everything seemed designed to blend and disappear.

"The Security Center," Gabe said with a grimace. "There's something about this place..."

I nodded slowly. Some indescribable quality that reeked of foreboding clung to the building. Perhaps the way the trees reached over everything like clawed hands, or the lack of windows or visible doors.

"Jake spends most of his time here. He watches out for us all, makes sure we avoid detection if anyone slips up or makes a mistake. He's done a lot for us. He's assigned you a job here, too, so he can keep an eye on you."

There was no door. I stared at the wall in confusion as Gabe stepped up to it.

The ground opened up beneath him, and my heart lurched.

"Gabe—!"

"It's all right," he said, flashing me a terse smile. "Just follow me. It's how we get inside." He paused. "And remember, I'm Garrett here."

I approached the gaping hole carefully. Sharp edges disappeared into a pit of blackness. I saw that Gabe stood on a small platform. I stepped onto it, my legs wobbling, and then we dropped into blackness.

SIXTEEN

WE DESCENDED WITH a thunderous whoosh and a rush of air. My stomach tumbled, and I squeezed my eyes shut, and then Gabe was tugging at my hands and a light was blinding me. I lifted my chin, brushed my fingers down the front of my itchy garment, and pretended I wasn't terrified as I followed him down a narrow stone corridor. The roof above our heads had shut, closing out the forest and the sky full of stars.

We were underground now.

The sound of our movements echoed through the passage. Lights danced overhead on a string, casting shadows, and I realized they were lanterns. The corridor smelled of metal and dirt. My pulse quickened as we turned a corner and I heard the low shriek of machinery, like the whisper of a nightmare. The metallic squeal almost sounded like the cry of a Watcher, and a shiver darted down my spine.

We turned another corner. A series of doorways lead right and left from the hall, and inside the rooms beyond, employees hunched over boxes with flickering lights or talked quietly. One man lifted his head when he saw us approach, and I recognized him as the man called Jake. He muttered something I couldn't hear to the person beside him, and then he moved swiftly to greet us outside in the corridor.

"Ah, the new swabber," he said loud enough that anyone curious would overhear and be satisfied. His gaze flicked over me curiously, and I had the impression that he never missed a single detail when he looked at something. I felt naked. "Garrett, isn't it?" Jake asked, as if he barely knew us. "And you are called Lila, yes?"

I nodded. My new name sounded so strange.

"Here," he said, throwing a glance over his shoulder at the room behind him. "I'll show you where the supply closets are."

We stepped down the hallway and descended a set of stairs. Lights flickered overhead and made our shadows leap. When we reached the bottom of the stairs, Jake opened a door and led us through another corridor. A massive steel door stood at the end of the hall, outlined in red. A sign above the door proclaimed CAUTION: AUTHORIZED ENTRANCE ONLY in bold white letters. Jake checked a device on his wrist and then led us to the door. It hissed open when he laid a hand against the side, and we stepped after him into a dark room. I heard echoes reverberate through the air and smelled dust and the faint scent of oil and leather. I could see nothing beyond the faces of my companions and a sliver of stone floor that vanished into the darkness looming above and around us. But wherever we were, it was cavernous.

"We can talk safely here," he said, rubbing a hand across his face, and then he dropped it and looked at me.

"Garrett said you had something important to tell me," he said. "A message."

"Yes," I said, moistening my lips with my tongue. "From Atticus."

Jake didn't change expressions when he heard the name, but his shoulders stiffened slightly, and he shifted his weight. "Go on."

I drew in a deep breath. "First, your place of origin?"

His expression never wavered. "I'm from Eos, originally."

It was Jacob, then. Relief flowed through my veins. I reached into my pocket and produced the envelope. I handed it to him. "I've brought the PLD," I whispered. "And this letter. It's a list of names..."

"PLD?" His forehead wrinkled as he accepted the envelope and turned it over in his hands.

"Portable Locomotion Device...a means to return home."

"Return home?" His mouth fell open, and he stared at me and then at Gabe as if for confirmation.

"To our time," Gabe said.

"You can't be serious. That's impossible. The gate doesn't yet possess the capabilities to return us to our own time; they haven't yet been invented..."

"That's why I brought the PLD," I interrupted. "It is from the future, so it does have the capabilities. It will work when the other gate won't. It will take those who are needed back to our time."

"And you're sure this is even possible?" He laughed in disbelief, but I saw the way his eyes narrowed and his mouth thinned. He was thinking about it now. The possibilities. The realities. What it would mean for him, for the fugitives.

"It's possible," I assured him.

He hesitated, remembering a detail. His eyes narrowed an almost imperceptible amount as he faced me. "You said 'those who are needed' will return?"

I licked my lips. "That is my message. That is what Atticus instructed me to say...what I came to deliver to you."

He took the envelope I'd given him and ripped it open. He scanned the list.

"Atticus says only those are to return, and you are to ensure that it is so."

I could see Jacob was turning the facts over in his head—who he would have to leave behind. A muscle in his jaw twitched, and then his eyes shuttered, and he nodded. "I see. Yes. Of course."

Beside me, Gabe was stiff and unreadable, but I could tell he didn't like it either. I felt miserable.

"Tell me what must be done," Jacob said.

"We must wait until the right time," I explained. "Two weeks. Then, we'll be able to make the jump back."

"Does anyone else know about this?"

"No one," I said. "Except me and...Garrett." I looked at Gabe and then away. "And he can be trusted."

Jacob nodded. "Where is the PLD now?" he asked.

"Safe." I said the word firmly, to signal that I wasn't yet ready to hand it over.

He seemed to accept this answer, and the understanding that I was not going to give it to him—not yet. "Good. Keep out of trouble, and try to avoid attracting too much attention to yourself. I'll keep an eye on you and speak to the others."

A clatter in the passageway just beyond startled us all. Jacob stepped back, putting a little distance between us. He raised his voice slightly. "This room is off-limits during the evening and morning shifts, do you understand? It's very important."

"I understand, sir," I said just as loudly.

A man poked his head in and spotted us. "Jake," he said to Jacob. "We need you upstairs. There's a situation." His gaze drifted over me absently. Beside me, Gabe reached out and touched my arm. It was an unconscious movement, but a protective one. A curious tingle shot through me, and I looked at him sharply. But he wasn't looking at me.

"You'll have access to the Security Center from now on," Jacob said to me after the dark-haired man had vanished. "So I can keep an eye on you and so you can pass any further information to me if needed. Your security clearance has been increased to allow it. I saw to that earlier. But we can't appear to be too close, to be friends. We can't have anyone linking us together. So I won't speak with you unless necessary."

"I understand," I said.

"Good. Now, I must go." He ushered us toward the door, and it hissed shut behind us, closing away that strange cavernous room of darkness and dust from sight

181

and leaving us alone in the corridor once more. He slipped away, leaving Gabe and me alone. Suddenly, my mouth was dry of words, and I couldn't quite meet his eyes. The memory of the way he'd touched me moments before lingered like the slightly bitter aftertaste of sugar, and I crossed my arms and rallied my emotions into a center of focus and calm.

I had more important things to do than worry about my feelings for this boy.

"Come on," he said. "I'll show you the supply closets."

~

We left the Security Center under the hush of darkness. The moon had moved higher in the sky, and silver light painted the path the color of ice so it looked like a frozen river weaving through the forest. Gabe and I followed it silently, walking side by side and breathing the same air as we each occupied our own thoughts. I was very aware of his shoulder, his arm, his dangling hand only inches from mine. He didn't look at me, and I didn't look at him, and I cursed the effect he had on me. But I couldn't deny the truth of it, either.

When we reached the top of the hill that looked down on the workers' village that would someday be Iceliss, my village, he finally spoke.

"I'm sorry I couldn't trust you with my secret before," he said. "But I hope you can trust me now."

I turned to look at him. My breath snagged in my lungs. My palms tingled.

"There are dangers here," Gabe said. "You've walked into something tangled."

"Dangers?"

"I don't know who to trust," he said. "I think I trust Jake, and there are a few others, but...there are many people who want many things, Lia. Be careful. That device you've brought—many people could want to get their hands on it. Keep it safe."

"I will," I said.

He finally raised his eyes to mine. An arrow of feeling shot through me, from my stomach to my toes, and I shivered. He lifted one hand and brushed my cheek, a caress so light it felt almost like wind. I sighed. He dropped his hand left me, heading for the men's quarters.

I continued on alone, moving through the warm, starlit blackness, listening to the whisper of wind through the trees behind me and smelling the scent of earth and mushrooms and sun-warmed flowers cooling in the night. A swirl of emotions simmered in my chest. Confusion, concern, apprehension...anticipation. I could still feel the place on my cheek where Gabe had touched me. It reminded me of Adam, and a similar touch on my face, and there was a throb of something in my heart— the cousin of pain, perhaps, but not quite pain itself.

I stopped before the barracks. I needed to think. I needed to plan before I faced anyone else, before I went into that strange, cold, brightly lit place and tried to shut out thoughts of my family and coax my body into sleeping. I found a moss-covered boulder at the edge of the building that faced the forest, and I sat on it and pulled my knees up to my chin.

Gabe and Jacob both had warned of danger, of people who could not be trusted. But neither of them had alluded to who these people might be. I could feel the threads of suspicion that ran through the whole compound tightening around me like invisible nets. My mind ran through the only people I had met. Claire? Juniper?

Gabe, at least, seemed to suspect that there might be trouble.

I needed to be very cautious.

Fatigue tugged at my eyelids and made my arms and legs feel heavy as stones. I was about to slip from the rock and head toward the door when a faint sound met my ears.

A shriek like knives against stone.

I froze.

At the edge of the tree line, a flicker of movement as faint as the flutter of an eyelash caught my attention. I held still, not breathing, not lifting a finger from the rock. I strained against the darkness, searching every shadow as my heart tumbled. My pulse beat a desperate rhythm in my head.

Nothing.

I sighed, sagged. I pushed myself from the rock.

And then—

The sound came again, a screech that made every hair on my body rise.

The sound of a Watcher. I would know it anywhere. I had spent my life straining for any hint of that sound. And I was caught like a rabbit, unable to move or even think. The night was hot and my fear was a shroud around me. I waited.

Silence seeped into the world again as my heartbeat slowed. Nothing moved against the trees. I was hallucinating, exhausted, hearing things. The difficulties of the day had muddled my mind.

Turning, I went inside to my room. I put thoughts of phantom Watchers and Adam Brewer and Ann in Astralux out of my head with the force of my iron-forged will, and miraculously, I fell asleep as soon as my neck relaxed against the pillow and my eyes shut.

SEVENTEEN

I SPENT THE next seven days grimly trying to smoothly navigate the bewildering world I'd been thrust into. I returned daily to work at Echlos—or the Labs, as everyone in this time called the white buildings that housed the gate—and mopped more shining floors until they gleamed like glass beneath my boots. Workers in white robes flowed around me, their faces somber and their mouths muttering to each other in whispers, but because of my olive garments and the mop in my hand that marked me as a swabber, no one looked my way. I relished the invisibility, because it made my job a thousand times easier. I kept my eyes open, absorbing everything I could from this fascinating place as I worked. I had already discovered many things on my own—like the fact that there were no horses here, at least not in this place. All the vehicles moved on their own, propelled by mysterious power much like the airships and trains of Aeralis, although these vehicles of the Ancient Age moved even more swiftly and silently than anything Aeralian. I'd also discovered that this place was completely isolated—the Compound, as they called it, was far from the cities of the south. The only people who lived in the village were workers for the

Labs or the Security Center or other places connected to the Compound. We were isolated, remote, just like in my time.

Travelers came through the gate at times, although few people seemed to want to stay here, and few remained long. The only arrivals I saw were men and women in dark red uniforms trimmed with black, people with dark hair and solemn faces and unsmiling, flat mouths. They walked the halls at a brisk pace, not stopping to make way for me or anyone else. They moved with the authority that spoke of people used to being silently accommodated, and the swabbers and other workers scurried away from them like mice. Only the people in white robes did not cower at their approach, I noticed. The red and black uniformed people seemed irritated by this.

The swabbers said nothing and only whistled to each other in lilting tunes while they worked, but other workers were not so tight-lipped. The people in the white coats were the ones who built the gates, I soon learned, and the ones who maintained the one here. They were scientists, inventors, geniuses brought from all over the world to labor here in this secluded place. They worked on other inventions, too—devices for convenience and health. The people in the red uniforms were here because of the health inventions. There were murmurs about "the Sickness," furtive glances among some of the workers and whispered words.

I wondered what was happening. What was this Sickness?

No one would speak of it. Not in enough detail that would give me any clues.

Almost every minute of the day, when I wasn't worrying about the mission, my thoughts were on Ivy and Jonn back at the farm. Anxiety burned like a smoldering bed of coals in my chest, keeping me breathless and harried, and Adam and Ann were never far behind in my spiral of thoughts. But rumination did me little good, so I fought the thoughts, doing my best to focus.

Claire worked alongside me at times, but never spoke. I saw Gabe in fleeting glimpses. We rarely had time to speak, but every time our eyes met, my stomach felt tight and words that I wanted to say filled my mouth. The memory of his fingers brushing my cheek filled my head, and I didn't know what I wanted.

I understood his secrecy now. I couldn't fault him for it. The hurt from it had leaked away, leaving in its wake emotions I didn't understand. I felt older now. Tired. I had loved Gabe like I had never loved any boy before, but now my heart felt twisted, stretched, pulled apart into different directions. Because now when I looked at Gabe, another part of me whispered Adam's name. And yet, I still cared for Gabe.

I didn't know what to think.

Several times, I spotted Doctor Borde, but I was never close enough to speak to him. And however was I supposed to barter with him in order to get whatever Jonn wanted me to get from him?

Concerns plagued me.

Every evening, I worked alone at the Security Center cleaning hallways. I saw Jacob in passing, but true to his promise, he never looked at me or spoke to me. I tried to hover in the background, observing and picking up information about the world. Several times I passed the door to the room we'd spoken in, the one with the large sign that read CAUTION in bold white letters. I did not clean inside, however, because the doors were never unlocked and no one ever opened them for me.

On the seventh night after my arrival, a shadow fell across my path as I was making the trek to the Labs, and Gabe stepped from behind the corner of a building.

My skin prickled with awareness of him. We hadn't spoken or spent any time together since our last conversation at the top of the hill following our visit together to see Jacob at the Security Center. My cheek still burned with the memory of his fingers against it. A soft ache hummed in my chest and whispered in my blood as I raised my eyes to meet his.

"Hello," he said.

"Hello."

"How are you doing?" The words were soft, almost gentle. They were also shy.

"As well as can be expected," I said. The words felt furtive, exchanged like whispers of love, but we were all business. We were standing close enough to be touching. His hand almost brushed mine, and I could feel the heat of his shoulder near my chest. The air around us felt on fire, and inwardly, I burned.

Gabe's eyes were unreadable. His eyelashes shivered as he squinted around us. "The fugitives have a meeting again tonight."

"Am I welcome there?" I asked quietly.

"Of course. You are one of us now."

I had felt somewhat isolated. Claire avoided me. I hadn't seen Juniper since my arrival. I didn't know most of the fugitives by sight yet, but the ones I did recognize seemed reluctant to make my acquaintance or form any sort of friendships. I wondered if they were wary of associating themselves with me specifically for some reason, or if they were simply slow to grow close to newcomers.

"Accompany me," Gabe said, and it was a question even though he sounded so certain. I met his eyes, and I saw a spark of something there that looked like hope. My stomach twisted and I found myself nodding.

"I'll find you after the third meal," he promised, and then he slipped away and left me standing there alone.

We had not touched, but I felt shaken and warmed all the same.

~

We reached the basement room late, just as last time. Most of the fugitives were already seated in a circle, murmuring to the person seated beside them or staring off into space. Most looked tired, some unhappy. I wondered briefly how they would all react if I raised my voice and announced that they could all return home in a week. Would they be relieved? Did they even want to go back?

They were mostly Aeralians, I supposed. They'd been fleeing for their lives, and if they returned with me to the Frost, they would only be fugitives again. But surely they had families, friends. People who they would never see again if they remained here.

I didn't know what to think. The weight of my secret tugged at me, and I took a deep breath. Gabe put a hand on the small of my back to guide me toward an empty seat, and I noticed Claire noticing the gesture from her place at the edge of the group. She glanced away when she saw me looking, and her long hair brushed her hands as her head turned sharply to avoid me.

I sank into the chair and looked around.

A woman stood up and spoke briefly about changes in meeting times. A few people protested, but most nodded in weary agreement. There seemed to be little official to talk about—the gathering seemed more for support than anything else.

They began telling their stories.

A man stood first. He shuffled his feet nervously, his eyes darting around. A long scar traced a path down his left cheek and ended at his neck. He traced it with his fingers as he spoke. "I was in southern Aeralis," he said. "The soldiers took my whole family when we wouldn't support the overthrow of the king. As far as I know, they are still in prison. Thorns operatives rescued me off a prison wagon and brought me here."

The next person to stand, I saw, was Juniper. He grinned at us, but pain lingered behind his expression. "I barely remember my life before the jump," he said. "I was so scarred up when I got here." He pulled down the edge of his collar, and I saw the web of scar tissue crisscrossing his chest. "But I remember the soldiers beating me with the butts of their guns." He touched the back of his head. "Had a cut here as wide as my finger. Miracle I survived at all."

My stomach turned at the sight of his scars. Would any of these people want to go back with me?

A woman spoke next, a story of dead children and a broken heart.

Claire stood after the woman had sank into her seat. She brushed at her long red hair with shaking fingers, looked around the room, and licked her lips. Then, she shook her head and sat down again.

"She always does that," Gabe murmured to me. He frowned. "She's never told her story."

A hand touched my shoulder. I looked up and saw Jacob. He motioned for me to follow him, and I left Gabe and went out with him into the hall.

"One week remains," he said as soon as we were alone. "Are you sure the device is safe?"

"It's safe," I said. "Have you made all the arrangements for those who are coming back with us?"

"I am working on that," he said. "I will contact you the day before so we can meet and make final preparations. Until then, continue as you've been doing, avoid attracting undue attention, and keep this quiet."

"I will."

Jacob started to say something else and stopped. He frowned, shook his head, and started toward the room with the others. He stopped. "What if we missed the jump next week?" he asked lightly. "What then?"

"We'd go at the next time," I said. "But we aren't going to miss it."

He nodded and stepped through the doorway. I remained alone in the hall, staring after him.

The door behind me opened and closed. I turned slightly, just enough to see who had joined me. It was Gabe.

"Jake seemed displeased," he observed, moving to my side and shoving his hands in the pockets of his garment.

I shrugged, because I didn't know what was going through the leader's head, and because I didn't really want to talk about that at the moment. Gabe's closeness was making it hard to think about Jacob, but I struggled to keep my mind on task. "We have only a week left," I said. "I think he's feeling the pressure of the...restrictions."

"You mean who we are supposed to bring back?"

I fiddled with the edge of one of my garment pockets.

Neither of us seemed to want to discuss it, so we didn't.

"How is your family?" Gabe asked. "Jonn...Ivy...?"

"Jonn's health is better. He's almost happy. And Ivy is growing like her namesake." Talking about them left a sweetness on my tongue that tasted bitter after the words faded. I sucked in a deep breath and blinked. "I hope they are well."

"I'm sure they are. They are strong," he said. "Just like you."

Our gazes connected. Mine stuttered away, but his was confident and sure. He took a step closer to me.

My heartbeat scrambled. I felt like a colt—skittish, ready to bolt.

"I've missed you," he said quietly. It was a confession. He dropped his head and then raised it again, gazing at me as if looking for any signs of condemnation, as if he expected them. "I've missed you so much."

I didn't dare speak. If I spoke a word, I might shatter this moment. I kept my lips shut and my eyes trained on his.

"Every single day I've been gone, I've thought of you. I've dreamed about you every single night. And I know we had made no promises...I know we have not spoken for each other, but—I've never felt about anyone the way I feel about you," he said. The admission came out of him painfully, almost brokenly. "I admire your strength, your intensity, your intelligence. You are the bravest person I know."

"Gabe—"

"I know you've moved on," he interrupted, rushing on. "I know I've been gone months. And as I said before, we've made no promises. And I was not honest with you. And—"

194

"I've missed you, too." The words ripped themselves from my throat. I hadn't meant to speak them, but they came out anyway. "I've tried not to think about you, but I..."

"Lia..." He closed the distance between us with a single step. His hands found my neck, his fingers slipped into my hair, and then he was kissing me. I wrapped my arms around his waist. I exhaled against his lips. I was lost and found at the same time, and he was the only anchor.

The kiss lasted seconds or days. I couldn't tell. All I could think about was the feel and taste of him, and the way I could feel his heart beating in his hands and through his chest. When we broke apart, he buried his face against my shoulder.

We stayed that way for a long time, drinking in the warmth of each other, relishing the precious closeness of another human being. I was drowning in the sensation. It had been so long since someone had taken me in their arms and whispered care and concern for me. My heart felt fragile and full, aching with the sudden rush of feeling.

The door jerked open behind us, and we jumped apart. A few of the fugitives streamed out. The meeting was over. Gabe and I exchanged glances, and without speaking we slipped upstairs with them and out into the night.

We walked back to the workers' barracks in warm silence. Where the previous silences between us had been walls, shutting out our feelings, this was like a blanket that wrapped us close and made us safe. Every time his hand brushed mine, I felt a burst of prickles over my skin. My mind was still a scramble, and my whole body had betrayed me by going dizzy and faint.

"We need to talk more about this," I said finally, in another burst of words that I hadn't planned to say. They leaped from my lips when we reached the door of the barracks. "I cannot...I don't want to...I don't know what I feel. Not anymore."

"We don't have to decide anything now," he said, and his eyes were luminous in the night. "Just let it be, Lia."

Before he left, he touched my face again and said my name. I shivered. I couldn't speak. I watched him walk away until he was gone and all that remained was the darkness of the streets and the sound of the wind in the trees behind me.

When I tried to sleep that night, I could not.

~

The mop in my hands rasped as it slipped over the tiled floor, and the steady sound of it had lulled me into a state of nervous tranquility as I worked in the Labs the next morning. Outwardly, I worked evenly and without expression. Inwardly, a jumble of things wrestled for my attention. The thought of the remaining days until the mission was complete ticked in my mind like a clock too loud in a silence. Ann and Adam were an ache in my chest whenever their faces crossed my mind. Jonn and

Ivy were a fear that pressed against me like the blade of a knife whenever I thought of their safety. And the kiss...

The kiss was a flutter of hope, a rush of heat, a trickle of shy longing. Every time I remembered the moment I'd spent in Gabe's arms the previous night, I felt hot and cold all over. Part of me wanted to allow myself to smile like a fool, and another part of me wanted to shake myself for such a silly impulse. *You mean nothing to him,* my mind whispered to me. *He is lonely. He simply wants comfort. He lied to you.*

But when I remembered the look in his eyes and the gentleness of his hands, those words were the ones that felt like lies.

Footsteps clipped against the tiles. Automatically, I pushed the bucket out of the way with my foot and pressed my back against the wall to give the approaching person room to pass. But instead, the footsteps slowed.

"Lila, is it?"

I raised my head and let my gaze slide up the figure of the person before me. I saw a white robe, a wrinkled mouth, a pair of shrewd, blue eyes. Doctor Borde.

My heart skittered.

"Yes," I said, the word a quiet admission in the stillness of the hallway. I glanced around. We were alone. No other stationaries, scientists, or even swabbers were visible the corridors. No other sounds floated down the passages to meet my ears.

"I'm Doctor Meridus Borde," the doctor said, accompanying his words with a nervous gesture of his hands. He looked at my face carefully, as if seeking any signs of recognition when he spoke the words. I gazed back evenly. I was frightened, but I wouldn't let him see that. I had looked Watchers in the face. I had watched men die in front of me. I would not flinch before this white-coated scientist from the past.

"So I've heard," I said.

The evenness with which I spoke seemed to focus him. He rubbed his chin with two fingers. His eyebrows pulled together. "We need to speak."

My pulse quickened at my opportunity, but I refused to be too eager. He had approached me. What did he want? What did he know? I kept my expression neutral, and I raised an eyebrow as if to say, *isn't that what we are doing?*

Borde chuckled nervously and shook his head. "Privately. Not here. It's not...safe."

"Safe?" My voice was calm, almost puzzled, as if I could not fathom how it could be unsafe. But my heart began to thud a rhythm against my ribcage, and sweat broke out across my back.

"I understand you have clearance at the Security Center," he said. "There is another building not far from it. If you follow the path past the field and through another stretch of forest, you'll find it. It's my personal lab, my place of private study. If you met me there tonight after your shift..." He paused. "There are things we need to discuss."

"Why should I come meet you somewhere all alone with no idea of what you want?" I said. My palms were almost too slick to hold the mop. "You could have inappropriate intentions. You could have ulterior motives. I don't know you. I have no reason to trust you or meet you somewhere alone."

He made a sound that was halfway between a laugh and a cough. "That is very wise of you, girl. But I have no intentions of that nature. Please. This is a very delicate matter."

"Give me some indication of what you want, then," I said.

His eyes narrowed slightly with sudden decision. He leaned close, so close I could smell the scent of soap on his cheeks and mint on his breath. "Perhaps you know this phrase," he said, and the next words he spoke turned my blood to ice.

"What woven secret will keep you warm?"

EIGHTEEN

THE WALLS, THE floor, everything faded away. I couldn't speak, couldn't move, couldn't breathe. The throb of my heart, the hiss of my breath—every detail crystallized as I stared at him in shock.

What woven secret will keep you warm? It was my father's riddle. The one he'd told me and my siblings when we were children, and the secret that had ultimately been the key to finding the PLD's secret location. How did this scientist from hundreds of years before my family's existence know of our riddle? Our specific riddle that referred to my mother's quilt— something that wouldn't be sewn into existence for another several centuries? Something that couldn't even exist as an idea, because the Frost it represented did not yet exist either. Our farm did not yet exist. How was this possible?

Meridus Borde drew back. His lips twitched in a wry smile as he observed the shock on my face.

"I take it by your expression that you know this phrase."

I couldn't speak.

"I'll see you tonight," he said. "Tell no one."

And then, he was gone, leaving me reeling in the wake of his words.

~

That night I slipped along the path through the forest to meet him, moving through the shadows to the sound of my own pulse in my ears.

I was alone.

I hadn't told anyone about what Doctor Borde had said to me. I hadn't seen Gabe, and of course I didn't trust Claire or any of the others. Even Jacob had been missing when I'd performed my nightly chores at the Security Center. The halls had been nearly empty, and as I worked and quietly panicked, I'd heard only the hushed murmurs of a few sleepy workers at their posts as they talked among themselves.

I moved through the darkness as I followed the path Borde had described. Around me, the trees reached out their tangled limbs like grasping fingers. The world looked so strange without its blanket of glittering white, even after a week of seeing it this way. The air was too hot, too close, too smothering. Sweat glistened across my forehead and beaded on my neck.

I'd only walked for a few minutes when I saw the lights in the distance. I rounded a curve in the path and there it was, a squat, rounded building huddled against a hill and shadowed by trees. A single light glowed from one of the windows.

I took a deep breath and let it out as I approached the door. I lifted my hand to knock, but it hissed open before I could, and a figure emerged.

Doctor Borde.

I squinted against the glare of light as my heart twisted with sudden apprehension. What if this was some kind of trap?

He motioned me inside. "I heard your approach because I have sensors along the path. No one can sneak up on me here," he explained, a note of pride in his voice.

I barely heard him, because I was gazing at the room we'd entered. It was surprisingly cozy, unlike nearly every other building on the compound. The walls were painted brown and covered with shelves that held boxes and books in heaps. Tables lined the room, similarly cluttered with objects that I couldn't identify by sight. A workshop.

"Can I get you anything?" Borde asked. "A drink, something to eat?"

My lips were dry, my hands damp. I brushed my fingers nervously down the front of my garment, and then realized I was showing my apprehension. I crossed my arms to keep from betraying myself further. I wanted to look strong, stoic. I wanted him to think I felt no fear. "Why don't we skip the pleasantries and get down to why I'm here?"

He motioned at a chair, but I was too nervous and anxious to sit, so I stood behind it. He sank into the one opposite, studying my face with an expression that looked almost like reverence.

"I don't know who you are," he said finally. "But I've been waiting for you."

"What do you mean, waiting for me?"

"How long have you been working here?" he asked instead of explaining.

"A week."

"Then you must have heard of the things we're struggling to decipher now. The Sickness."

Apprehension prickled my spine. I watched his face carefully, looking for clues of what he meant, what he wanted from me. Was he trying to trip me up, lure me into making a mistake? Was he trying to get me to reveal some vital clue, some piece of information? What did he even want from me? I needed to proceed carefully. And as soon as I saw an opportunity to twist the situation to my advantage, I needed to take it.

"I don't know much about the Sickness," I said finally. "I have only heard a few stories."

"I've only seen manifestations once or twice myself," he admitted. "We are isolated from it here, and we are safe, mostly. But the Sickness. It...changes people."

I waited for him to elaborate, but he didn't.

Borde studied my face again. "It's incredible," he murmured, almost involuntarily.

"What's incredible?" I asked.

He came to himself and shook his head. "Nothing. I ramble sometimes. It's one of my most endearing qualities."

He flashed me a cheeky grin, but I was not amused. He waited a beat and then sighed. "I have questions I want to ask you, but I cannot. Not yet. I am not sure I can trust you."

And I'm not sure I can trust you, I thought, but I didn't say that aloud. I simply waited for him to continue while my heart hammered in anticipation of what he might reveal. What could he possibly want from me? Why did he need to trust me? What questions did he have?

"Don't you have any questions for me?" Borde asked after a long pause in which we simply stared at each other, silently challenging each other to each reveal their hand first. "I've invited you here in the dead of night, under utmost secrecy, and now I cannot bring myself to even say anything. Surely you are baffled."

My lip curled slightly. So that was his game. Put the burden on me to make conversation, and see what I revealed? Clever, clever. I would not fall for such a trap.

"Perhaps you are lonely," I said. "And you are ashamed to admit it."

"Ah," he said. "A sound theory, maybe. But you are forgetting our conversation earlier. It would suggest that you know something else. That we both do."

The riddle. My heart sank. He'd known the riddle— how could he know the riddle?—and he'd seen my face when he spoke it to me. He knew it meant something to me, but I didn't have to tell him *what.*

Borde waited, but I said nothing else. Finally, he sighed. "I am in a terrible position, my girl," he said. "I am not sure who I can trust anymore."

I raised an eyebrow. First Gabe, now him. Was not a single person in this place trustworthy?

"So," he continued, "I am not sure what I can tell you. I must proceed with caution, because my work is of the utmost importance." He waited again, but still I said nothing. Finally, half his mouth quirked in a wry smile. "You're a cool one, aren't you?"

"So I'm told," I said.

He shook his head and muttered something under his breath, and then he rose with a grunt. "I've taken up enough of your time, my girl. We shall talk more later. Thank you for humoring me with this visit, unproductive as it may be."

Protest stirred inside me. I'd come, but I'd discovered nothing. What about the riddle. "Wait," I said quickly. Borde froze. Hope gleamed in his eyes and danced along the lines of his body as he turned.

"Yes?"

"The—the thing you said before." Tension knit into my muscles. I didn't want to say this, but I needed to know. I needed to find out something. "Where did you hear that?"

He gazed at me a long moment, making a decision. "In a journal," he said finally, and then paused again. "I...wait here."

He left the room, moving quickly, and I noticed he had the faintest limp. I sank into one of the chairs and looked around. Most of the objects spread across the tables were gadgets, strange pieces of technology that defied categorization or understanding on my part. On the table closest to me lay a slender metal pole with buttons running up and down the sides. Across the room, different colored liquids simmered in glass containers. The whole room smelled like pipe smoke and dust and something sharp and acrid.

Most of the shelves in the room were filled with loose papers or boxes, but one shelf in the far corner held a collection of dusty books. I rose from my chair and approached it, casting a quick glance over my shoulder to see if Borde was coming back. He wasn't.

I reached the shelf and peered at the titles. Most sounded ponderous and academic, and some were simply unfamiliar fictions, but one snagged my eye. My heart thumped painfully as I stared, absorbing what I saw.

The Winter Parables.

My heart tumbled. My parents had owned the same book. Gabe had found and read it during his stay at the farm, and he'd left me a letter in it after he left. It was in my room now, back in the farmhouse in the Frost. It was buried beneath my woolen socks in the top drawer of my bureau.

I reached out one finger to touch the spine. The words glittered on it, taunting me. *The Winter Parables.* The title seemed almost prophetic, given the future of snow that awaited this place.

Footsteps echoed behind me. Borde was returning. I stepped away from the bookshelves before he entered the room.

In his hands, he carried a leather notebook. He carried it close to his chest, almost as if it were a baby or some other fragile, precious object that he didn't want to relinquish. He sank into the chair opposite me and held the book on his lap. I could tell he wanted me to demand answers, but instead, I waited for him to explain.

"The phrase I spoke to you," he began. "What woven secret will keep you warm?"

I nodded. I kept my face carefully composed despite the riot of nervousness dancing in my stomach.

"I read that phrase here, in this." He ran a finger over the cover of the notebook. His mouth twisted with a painful smile as he ran his thumb across the corner of the pages, making them purr.

I wanted to reach out and snatch it from his hands. How could this notebook hold a riddle that my family had invented? Unless my father had taken it from some other place, appropriated an old riddle into something specific that related to his family alone? That must be it. But why then did this man repeat it to me, looking for a reaction? What did he know? What did he hope to discover?

Was this what Jonn wanted me to get from him?

The questions burned inside me.

Borde made a sound of frustration deep in his throat. He rose from his chair and gestured restlessly with one hand. "I cannot trust you. I cannot reveal what I know, not yet. And it is late."

"I..." I had nothing to say. It was true. He did not trust me and I did not trust him. We were at an impasse. And perhaps this was all some clever ruse on his part, some trap to make me talk. I couldn't be sure.

I had to be careful.

"I want something from you, too, but I cannot trust you either."

He stared at me a long time. "I don't know what to think of you," he said.

I laughed.

"Can you find your way back to the workers' barracks?" he asked.

"I know the path," I said.

"Good." He paused. "Be sure to stay on it. And move swiftly—take care that you are not seen."

Again, the mysteriousness of his words prickled my spine. I nodded and went to the door. He opened it for me. I went out into the night. We exchanged no goodbyes. He simply watched as I stepped into the warm darkness and disappeared from his sight.

The forest around me hummed with quiet as I traveled down the path. The scents of pine and dirt reached my nose on a breeze that stirred my hair and made the cuffs on the sleeves of my work garment flutter. What was Borde up to? He had singled me out and repeated a riddle I'd known since infancy, then asked me to meet him here. He'd shown me a notebook but refused to give me any further information, citing a lack of trust. What was he afraid of? Who was he afraid of? Or was this all some elaborate trap designed to draw me out?

A sound interrupted my thoughts. The faintest rasp, like metal against stone. I stopped.

I knew that sound.

Reflexively, I scanned the forest. My pulse pounded in my throat. My breathing was too loud in my ears as I strained to hear. The shadows lay deep and still all around me. To my left, a tree branch quivered. I heard nothing.

Then—

The screech was loud and close, almost on top of me, and I ran without thinking. Years of practice spurred me forward to seek cover in the trees. Limbs whipped at my face and snagged my clothes, but I didn't stop until I'd tumbled to safety beneath a boulder. Pine needles bit into the skin of my palms. My hair stuck in clumps to the sweat on my neck. I lay sprawled, breathing hard and searching for signs of movement.

And I saw it.

A motion, a curl of activity, a single stretch of fluid movement in the dark. Something shifted, stirred, emerged.

Moonlight glittered along a wicked-looking spine and glistened against a neck. Red gleamed from searching eyes. A mouth gaped, teeth sparkled.

A Watcher.

NINETEEN

"WHAT HAPPENED?" CLAIRE blurted in horror as she peered at my face the next morning.

"I ran into a branch," I replied, which was the truth. I was unable to think of a more suitable excuse as I gingerly touched the lacerations across my cheek, because I hadn't slept. I could barely think.

I knew what I'd seen.

My chest tightened at the memory. I'd remained in the underbrush until the creature had passed. There had been no denying what it was. The teeth, the glowing red eyes, the vicious chugging of its hot breath. I'd returned back to the town at a stumbling run, vulnerable and terrified without any snow blossoms or embroidered cuffs to protect me. If the monsters attacked, I would have nothing. For the first time in my life, I was completely vulnerable against the creatures, and the sensation terrified me.

"If you see Garrett," I said to Claire, "tell him I must speak to him at once."

~

Gabe found me as I was finishing my work at the Labs.

"What's wrong?" he asked, drawing me aside to the privacy of an alcove and taking my face in both his hands. His touch was so gentle that my eyes almost prickled with tears. "Claire said—"

"I saw a Watcher in the woods," I said.

He shook his head as he probed the cuts on my cheeks carefully. "You were imagining things. You heard the transports, perhaps. They are loud and sudden. Or one of the vehicles—"

"I wasn't imagining anything. I know exactly what I saw. I've seen it multiple times. The red eyes. The massive teeth. The claws..."

"Lia," he said, his tone coaxing. "It's impossible. There are no Watchers here."

"You're wrong," I said. "I saw one last night in the woods."

"Where? Near the Labs? The Security Center?"

"Not quite, it was near..." I stopped. I couldn't tell him about Borde. Not yet. I needed to think about that a bit more. "It wasn't far from it, though."

I could see him sorting through things in his head, probably trying to choose the most gentle and soothing response. It rankled me. He was trying to assuage what he thought was panic on my part, female hysterics because of the pressure.

"You're exhausted," he said finally. "You're still recovering from your jump. It's only been a week. You've had a huge transition—"

"Gabe," I interrupted. "I didn't imagine this. Pretending that I made it all up does nothing."

"I'm sorry," he said. "But there are no Watchers here. It has to be something else."

"Or you're wrong about that."

He sighed. "Listen. What do you want me to do?"

"I don't know. I just...I don't know what it means. And I need some snow blossoms."

"All right." He gave me a tired smile. "We'll find you some snow blossoms."

I still felt annoyed, because he was humoring me. I knew what I'd seen. There were Watchers here. I was sure of it.

~

We found the snow blossom bushes. They grew wild at intervals around the town and in some of the nearby fields, but the greatest abundance of them grew in a lush hollow between two hills. The flowers covered the hills like snow, and for a moment I almost felt as if I was back home in the Frost. In the distance, the white roof of a shimmering building curved and swooped in fantastic shapes, like a bird poised for flight. A fountain sparkled before a curving road, and in the distance I could see glimmers of the rails that carried the fast, silent trains. It was all alien to me, a magical and frightening landscape of another world.

"What is that place?" I asked.

"That's the house of the Compound director," Gabe said. "I work as a gardener here sometimes. Pretty, isn't it?"

Pretty? I snorted. It made the village Mayor's house seem like a shack in comparison. But that made me think of Ann, and thinking of Ann brought a stab of pain. I steered my mind back to the snow blossoms. "There are so many here."

"The snow blossom is actually the Compound symbol, you see. The director's wife chose it. And they aren't native to this area," he explained as I plucked a few fragrant blossoms from the stems and held them to my nose. "They actually don't do so well here in the heat, but they're the Compound director's wife's favorite flower, so she had them brought here. They're transplanted from colder regions, where they were engineered to withstand extreme temperatures. Here, they grow like wild flowers. They're spreading everywhere."

So this was the origin of our precious blossoms. The whims of a rich man's wife. I squinted again at the magnificent house in the distance. That woman, whoever she was, had no idea what her gardening would produce 500 years in the future. She had no idea that one day children in ragged cloaks would bind these flowers around their necks and wrists to keep them safe from red-eyed monsters that roamed a frozen wasteland.

The thought made me melancholy, wistful, and a bit annoyed.

I strung a few of the blossoms on a string and hung them around my neck, then plucked a few more to take back to my room. I would hang them to dry, and make more necklaces later.

When I raised my head, I found Gabe looking at me. His gaze was soft, open, and I felt suddenly nervous about what he might say. "Have you spoken to Jacob since the meeting night?" I asked.

"Not really," he said. "He's been busy. The Security Center has a new project they've been working on. With the increase in visits from the southern cities, they've needed extra security. Most of his time and attention has been focused there. The Compound is taking on new responsibilities when it comes to managing the Sickness...they are seeking a cure."

"Do they find it?" I asked softly.

He laughed, but it was a helpless sound. "I don't know. Our history books don't extend this far back," he said. "But if they do, it becomes lost. No one knows how to cure it in our time, you know."

"Can we do anything to help them?"

He shook his head.

I felt strange, restless. We were out of place here, watching these people struggle, knowing it would all fall to pieces before long but not knowing why.

After gathering enough flowers, I headed for the Labs and my duties. The scent of the snow blossoms hanging from my neck surrounded me as I swabbed the floors of the Labs, making them shine even more brightly than they already did. Outwardly, I might look tranquil, but inside my head, I was turning over the various things I'd learned and seen in the last two days.

I hadn't seen Doctor Borde again yet. I needed to approach him, set up another meeting. What was the meaning of that journal he'd showed me? How had he known my father's riddle? I had so many questions, and there were no answers in sight. And Jonn and Ivy—were they safe? Were they fed? I tried to tell myself that Everiss would take care of them, but the thought afforded me little comfort. And Adam was not there to help. Worry twisted in my stomach like a snake.

I was so preoccupied with my thoughts that I almost didn't hear the clip of boots against the floor. Just in time, I dragged the bucket out of the way and pressed my back against the wall as a line of red and black-uniformed individuals rounded the corner, almost at a run. Their faces were the color of whitewash, and their mouths were mashed in thin lines.

Among them, two of the uniformed men half-dragged, half-carried a moaning figure. Perspiration dotted a purple-hued face and saliva streamed from cracked lips. Hands clawed at nothing. I couldn't even tell if the sufferer was a man or a woman. The figure writhed, panting like an animal. Shivers descended my spine and tingled in my hands. Was it the Sickness?

The group turned another corner and vanished. All that remained was a few drops of spittle on the floor, and the fading outline of footprints in the wet slick on the floor where I'd been mopping.

A knot of foreboding doubled in my chest.

~

That night in the dining hall, a current of unrest simmered in the air. The workers muttered and cast dark glances at each other as they scarfed down their food. The tension in the room slipped into my blood and made my muscles tight. I sat with Claire. She seemed similarly affected; she barely touched her food. We didn't speak.

Behind us, I heard two workers whispering.

"I heard they brought in a man today. An infected man."

"He's under quarantine," another murmured. "They have it under control."

"Why did they bring him here? He's got the Sickness!"

"There's no proof of that. They're denying it."

"No, no, it's true. Some of the swabbers in the Lab saw them."

"I don't believe it."

I remembered the purple face and strangled cries of the infected person. I shut my eyes and took another bite of my food. Despite my lack of appetite, nourishment was not a thing to squander. There were only five days left until we would jump back to my time, and I needed to absorb every bit of strength that I could from this place while I was here.

When Claire and I left the dining hall and headed to our respective work stations, I saw gray-robed workers climbing from a vehicle at the gate to the town. They wore masks over their noses and mouths, and gloves on their hands. A trickle of something like panic dripped into my stomach, but I shoved the feeling away. There was no time to panic. I couldn't afford to lose my head now.

The hallways of the Labs buzzed with frantic activity. White-robed professionals whispered in doorways, and workers hurried back and forth with unreadable expressions plastered across their faces. A few swabbers slipped through the confusion, silent as usual. I fiddled with my mop and watched everything from a safe distance, unnoticed and unobserved. When no one was watching me, I set off down one of the halls toward the place where the scientists worked.

I scanned the words on the wall. Signs marked where each scientist's room was. Finally, I saw Borde's name. My heart thudded. I glanced around to be sure no one watched, and then I put my finger to the knob. I expected it to be locked, but the door opened.

I slipped inside and left a note on his chair. I didn't sign it, but I knew he would know I was the one who had left it.

As I left the room, I was almost knocked over. Two red and black-uniformed women clipped past me at a fast rate, and something about their expressions snagged my interest. They were heading for the gate chamber, which was only a few corridors away.

After a moment's hesitation, I followed. The doors to the gate bay hissed open to admit them, and I slipped inside just before the panels shut again.

The room echoed with bustle. The uniformed women crossed the vast expanse that lay between me and the gate. They did not look back at me. Far away, I could see a few white-coated scientists waiting. One paced, the other stood with his arms crossed and his head tipped to one side. My stomach turned over when I realized it was Doctor Borde, and I took a step back, but he didn't look in my direction. I was probably too far away for him to even notice me.

The gate was live. Threads of light glimmered along the ground and sparkled in the seams of the structure. A sizzle shot through the air and crawled over my exposed skin, making my hair prickle. I tasted the flavor of metal when I inhaled.

Sudden light spiked from the gate's mouth, and a pulse of sound shivered through the air like an exhale. A retinue of figures was suddenly crouched in the landing area, fresh from a jump, most of them with hands over their faces. Jumping was not pleasant for most, as I now knew from experience.

One man stood upright, seemingly unaffected by the disorienting effects of travelsickness. Long hair cascaded over his shoulders in an inky wave, and he wore white gloves and a uniform of deep purple. As I watched, Doctor Borde and the other scientist approached him.

I guessed these people were from the colonies, or some other such place.

"You shouldn't be here," a voice said at my elbow, and I jerked around.

It was the dark-haired man I'd seen before, on my first day at the Labs. Doctor Gordon, someone had called him. He stood a few feet away, regarding me curiously. His eyebrows arched, and his mouth curled in a challenging smirk. He wore the white robes of a scientist.

"I'm a swabber," I said, fumbling with my badge.

He sniffed. "Swabbers never talk."

"I do."

"Well, he said, "you're not cleared for this meeting. All staff was dismissed. Didn't you hear?"

"No," I said, refusing to blink.

"Well, now you've heard."

I sneaked a last glance at the scene by the gate as I left. The man in the purple uniform had stepped from the landing pad and was greeting Doctor Borde. He had a haughty, cold expression, as if he were a prince tasked with cleaning a garbage pit. I couldn't see Borde's face because he had his back to me, but I heard someone mention the Sickness, and the word floated like a curse in the air. Then the doors slid shut, and I was alone in a glimmering hall, my heart hammering against my ribs and my skin flushed.

Only four more days till the jump.

~

A whistle laced the air and all the swabbers around me lifted their heads. They drifted away, leaving me alone. I never ran away when the rest of them did. I kept cleaning, kept company by my thoughts, until a voice interrupted them.

"I got your note. We need to speak."

I lifted my head and saw Doctor Borde standing in front of me. His hands twisted together. He blinked rapidly.

"Now?" I glanced around at the surrounding halls. All the other swabbers were gone. It was only me and the scientist.

"Now. Come with me."

He strode off without waiting for me to agree to anything. I hesitated, but not for long. He turned the corner and I was at his heels, following his fluttering coat down a corridor and into a dark room. Not his office. A closet. My head bumped a low-hanging light, and my shoulder grazed a shelf before he found the switch and fumbled with it to make the lantern dangling overhead gleam.

"There isn't much time." He turned to face me as soon as the space was illuminated. "I saw you in the Arrival Bay yesterday," he said. "When the Health Inspector came."

I didn't nod or smile or frown. I gave away nothing by my expression. Borde hissed out another sigh. "You seek to trap me," he said, rubbing his temples with both hands.

"I just want to know what you want from me."

He pressed a fist to his mouth. I could read the confliction in his eyes. "I think...I think you aren't from here."

Panic blossomed in my stomach, but I kept my face carefully controlled. "I'm not," I said.

Borde's eyebrows drew together sharply.

"I'm...I'm from the coast," I said quickly.

"Oh." He hesitated, stopped. "I...that's not what...no, no, I've taken too much of your time."

"Wait," I said, grabbing his sleeve before he could slip away. "There is something...I need something from you. If you have questions for me, I'll answer them in exchange for it."

He paled. "For what?"

"This." I produced the paper Jonn had given me and handed it to him. He unsealed it and scanned the contents, then exhaled. He raised his eyes to mine. "This all you want?"

"Yes," I said firmly.

"All right. Meet me again at my private quarters, the same as before. I'll have what you need waiting for you."

"Wait," I said, before he could go. "Why did that Health Inspector come here? What's going on?"

"My girl," Borde said, "haven't you heard? We had our first instance of the Sickness."

TWENTY

THREE DAYS UNTIL the jump, and everyone was frightened. Whispers swirled like smoke through the entire Compound, polluting the atmosphere and breathing fear into everyone's lungs. The murmur on everyone's lips was *quarantine.* Nobody knew anything solid. Nobody knew anything at all.

Except me.

Doctor Borde had said it himself. The Sickness was here.

I moved as if in a dream. The shining halls of the Labs and the dark, warm forests on the way to the Security Center flowed around me like delusions. My control was slipping, and the thoughts in my head moved constantly between the mission, my loved ones back home, and the Sickness. What if one of us caught it? What if we took it back to the Frost?

That night, I slipped from the barracks and set out toward the Security Center. My blood burned in my veins as I jogged, because I had a mission. After I was finished, I was going back to Borde's private research lab. Fear simmered in my blood, but I pushed the emotions away. There wasn't time to get distracted.

I was so absorbed in my thoughts that I barely heard the snap of branches. I'd grown lax in my days of relative safety.

A hand grabbed me. I gasped, cursed, fell. Fingers pressed over my mouth and eyes stared into mine. "Don't scream," a voice hissed.

Jacob.

"Jake," I snapped. "I thought you were a Watcher." I picked up the broken snow blossom necklace from the ground and tossed it into the underbrush.

"Watcher?"

"The monsters," I said. "Surely you remember them from your passage through the Frost before you came here."

Something shifted in his gaze, a scuttle of understanding that hinted at something else, but it crawled away before I could analyze it or probe further. "Ah, yes," he said. "I remember. But they aren't—" He stopped. Apparently attempting to argue with me didn't matter right now.

"What do you want?" I brushed twigs and dirt from my uniform and swiped strands of hair from my eyes.

"We have to talk about the PLD," he said.

Suspicion barbed me. I raised my eyebrows faintly, showing my surprise but nothing else. Not my suspicion, certainly. "What about it?"

He hesitated. "The Sickness is here, Lia." He dropped the use of my fake name since we were alone, and his choosing to use my real name sharpened my attention. Whatever he was about to say, he was serious about it.

"Yes," I agreed.

He turned his head and looked into the shadows of the forest. He appeared to be choosing his words carefully, but finally he made a sound of frustration. He scrubbed a hand over his face. "I can't leave any of my people here."

"Your people?"

"The fugitives. The travelers. They are my people now. We've been a family for years. I've taken care of them. I can't leave them, not now. Not with the Sickness spreading, and everything falling apart..."

Atticus's orders returned to my mind. I saw his gaze in my mind, so cold and ruthless. Snake-like. His threats hovered in my memory. "I can't let you do that," I said automatically, but my mind was churning with thoughts. I understood his position. Of course I did. If I was in his place, I'd feel the same way. I knew without a doubt that if Ann and Adam and the rest were to be left behind...well, I would never do it.

But I had my orders, too. And there would be consequences for failure. We were at an impasse. So who would blink first?

I pressed my lips in a firm line. I was tough as the ice that coated our river, hardened by years of snow and wind and Watcher attacks. He would not crack me.

Jacob's eyes narrowed to slits as he saw my resolve. "I won't go if they don't."

I needed to think, to plan. And I wasn't going to do that on my feet, not in the dark like this when I was so on edge. "I have to get to the Security Center," I breathed. "We will talk about this tomorrow."

I didn't know if he'd let me go, but he nodded and stepped back. "Fine," he said.

I slipped up the path to the Center. My lungs hurt and my skin was shimmering with perspiration.

What now?

~

A few hours later, I knocked on Doctor Borde's door.

For one long, breathless moment I thought he wasn't going to answer, but then I heard the locks sliding. The door hissed open and Borde peered at me, his eyes red-rimmed and his hair in a snarl. His shirtsleeves were rolled up to his elbows, and a stain adorned the breast pocket, evidence of a late-night meal hastily consumed.

"You have what I asked for?" I asked.

"Yes," he said. "But...I just don't know if I can trust you. You have to make it worth my while to give it to you."

"All right," I said. "How?"

"Are you—are you working for Doctor Gordon?"

"What?" Confusion filled me. That mean scientist? "No. Why?"

225

Borde frowned, looking unconvinced. "A brilliant man...and my professional rival. I thought...well, never mind. Come in, Lila."

I drew in a deep breath and made a desperate gamble. "Actually, my name isn't Lila."

His hands stilled on the door.

"It's Lia. Lia Weaver."

His eyebrows pulled up sharply at the word *Weaver*, and his entire expression changed. He stepped back. "Come in at once and tell me everything."

I stepped across the threshold and into the room crammed with shelves and tables. The scent of something cooking met my nose. The door snapped shut behind me, and my heart pounded. Was I really going to do this? I had to proceed carefully. Give him just enough information that he gave me what I needed to know.

"Sit, sit," Borde babbled. "Let me get you some tea."

He scurried away, leaving me standing in the middle of the room. My legs trembled with a sudden attack of nerves, so I sank into one of the chairs he'd indicated. The fabric creaked and dust plumed from the arms as I sat down. Borde returned with a steaming cup in his hands. He handed it to me and then dropped into the chair across from mine.

"Please," he said. "Please continue."

I closed my fingers around the edges of the cup of tea in my palms and leaned forward. "First, what I asked for."

He nodded and jumped up again. He disappeared into another room and returned with a narrow white box made from a strange, light material. It was tightly sealed. He set it on the table beside my chair. "All exactly according to the instructions you gave me," he said, and licked his lips nervously. "Now..."

"Wait," I said. "I need some more information, too."

He was very still, as if I wielded a knife, and he was trying to calculate the best way to disarm me. "Oh?"

"The Sickness—what is it? What causes it? How do you catch it...how do you know if you're infected?"

He lowered his head for a moment, and his shoulders relaxed. My attention sharpened. He'd been expecting me to ask something else. What?

"I...this is classified information..."

"Tell me," I demanded.

He winced. "The Sickness can pass through the air or, if one is attacked by the infected, through the blood. Bites."

"Bites? As in...animals?"

"Some animals are unaffected and some..." he trailed off, and I understood. "Rats, for instance, are susceptible. Horses are not."

I waited for him to continue.

"The infected first experience nose bleeds, broken capillaries in the eyeballs, a reddening of the skin, bleeding gums. It only gets worse from there. Symptoms escalate into vomiting, coma, death. Less than twenty-five percent of the infected survive, and those who do are...changed."

"Changed? How?"

He shook his head. "We still don't fully understand it. Not yet."

"Is that why they brought that infected man here?"

He didn't answer.

Frustration bubbled up inside me, but I tamped it down and took a deep breath. This was the part where I had to proceed very carefully. I couldn't spook him—he was very nervous, clearly—and I couldn't give away too much.

"Is there any way to treat the Sickness?"

"Not that we have discovered," he admitted, and his eyes shifted to the left, focusing on the door. He frowned, but then the creases in his forehead eased as he looked back at me. "Your turn," he said. "You say your name is Lia, not Lila." He hesitated for so long that the silence grew too thick, almost suffocating. I wanted to scream, but I held my composure. Finally, Borde asked, "Where are you really from?"

The question hovered between us as foreboding as a weapon. I braced myself against the chair. I couldn't breathe. The words in my mouth burned on my tongue, but I forced them out. I felt the power of them charging the air as I spoke.

"I'm from here, actually. But I'm not...I'm not from this time."

Borde exhaled shakily.

I expected him to laugh or roll his eyes or demand that I leave. But he did none of those things. Instead, he wept.

He *wept.*

I half-rose from my chair. "Have you gone mad?"

"I'm fine," he muttered, swiping at his eyes with his right wrist. "Forgive me. I'm just—this is very overwhelming for me. I've wondered for so long..."

"Wondered what?" I demanded. My impatience was unraveling; I needed answers. I was running out of time.

"Yes, yes," he said to himself. "Of course. She probably came by way of the device, but why?"

She. He was talking about me. *The device.* Anxiety burned a hole in my stomach. What did he know? "Tell me," I said.

Borde lifted his head. His eyes flared with excitement. He clasped his hands together. "For some time now," he said, "I have been working on plans for a device. A device that will allow travel not simply through space, like the gates, but through time."

I held very still. "And?"

"I have not yet finished it. I am stuck. But I have the journal, and it proves that I will succeed one day."

The notebook he'd showed me before. The hairs on my neck rose. "Tell me about the journal, Borde."

He flinched at my sharp use of his name. "I...I don't know where it came from, actually. It is very old, it seems. The leather is cracked and faded. The pages are filled with scribbles, inscriptions...phrases that I do not understand."

"But what does that have to do with me?" He was rambling now. I had to make him focus.

Borde shook his head. He wasn't going to tell me. Not yet.

"What of the riddle?" I demanded.

Borde blinked. "Riddle?"

"What woven secret will keep you warm?" As the words left my lips, I shivered. It felt strange and wrong to speak them here, in this strange time so far from my home, my people, my Frost.

"It is written in the journal," he said. "Over and over again."

A shiver ran through my body. I rose from the chair and paced.

"What is the phrase?" he asked, searching my face.

"It is a riddle invented by my father," I said. "To entertain me and my siblings as children, and to...to communicate a secret about where a time travel device was located."

Borde's expression melted into pure amazement. His eyes widened and his mouth dropped open. "Oh," he breathed.

"Perhaps I've said too much," I said. "But you have not yet said enough."

"There is much I cannot say. It is secret, all my plans and progress—"

"Who else knows about the journal?" I interrupted.

"No one," he said. "I swear it. My wife knew it, but she is gone now. My children know nothing. My colleagues know nothing."

That made me feel safer. I stopped pacing to study him. He looked sincere. But I still wasn't sure that I could trust this man, although perhaps I had little choice. If

Jacob knew what I was doing—or Atticus—they would be furious. Perhaps worse.

But he had information, and I needed it. "Can I see this journal?"

Borde's hands stilled in his lap. He leaned back. "I...it is full of secret things. If you were a spy..."

"There might be things that I would know," I insisted. "Things I could understand."

Borde was shaking his head.

I tried to keep him talking. He'd been willing to converse about the Sickness, at least. "Can you tell me anything more about the Sickness," I said.

"Not much more is known," he insisted. "We are studying it, but...most of what we know is rumor and fantasy."

"How is it treated?"

"The victims are isolated so they cannot infect anyone else. As they progress through the stages of infection, they become disoriented, sometimes crazed. They attack others in some cases, biting and clawing and spreading the disease even faster than normal. A person who breathes the air of an infected might catch the Sickness. A bitten person is certain to. Those who are infected must be quarantined, kept under watch."

I breathed out slowly. "And if the disease doesn't kill them?"

"Then they are no longer susceptible to catching it again," he explained. "In fact, recovering victims of the Sickness are often physically stronger. The disease seems to fix many problems, things that might have otherwise been permanent damage. Eye disorders, autoimmune problems..."

I absorbed this. It was fascinating. "And I can carry the disease on my clothes, my body, even if I am uninfected?"

"Yes, although it spreads much faster through the infected."

We needed to get away as soon as possible, then. We couldn't risk staying any longer, no matter what Jacob wanted. My heart thudded. "Thank you," I said. "Now, I only need one more thing before I go."

He waited.

"I need to see the journal."

He shook his head. "I cannot. I am sorry, but I cannot trust you enough to reveal its contents to you. Not yet."

I made a small noise of frustration. Perhaps he thought he had weeks, months to observe me and determine my trustworthiness, but I had only days! And I could not tell him that. I could not reveal our scheduled departure to anyone else. It wasn't safe.

"Fine," I growled. "We shall talk of this again. Tell no one what I have told you."

"Of course not," he said. "No one shall know but me. And...and you?"

"Who am I going to tell?" I said, thinking that I dared not reveal what I'd done to Jacob. I wasn't even sure if I could tell Gabe. Not now, not yet. Perhaps once we were safe in the Frost.

I almost laughed at the notion that the Frost was safer than this place. But in some ways, it was. At least in the Frost, I knew the rules, I knew the way the world worked, and I knew how to navigate that world, dangerous as it might be.

"I have to go," I said. "But we will talk again."

I hoped it was true, because I needed to see that journal. I knew there were things he wasn't telling me. It had something to do with my family—but what?

I picked up the sealed container, the thing that held Jonn's secret, and left.

TWENTY-ONE

TWO DAYS UNTIL the jump, and I was a riot of nerves. My work passed in a blur. I moved like a dead woman through meals, through duties. Finally, after darkness had descended over the Compound, I paced the floor of my tiny room like a caged animal, making quiet noises of frustration as I tried to sort out the tangle of problems in my head. Jacob wanted to bring everyone. The Sickness made everything so much more complicated. And now Borde had a journal that held my family's secrets. I had to know what else it contained.

If it had one of my father's riddles, what else might the pages contain? The possibility burned inside me like a star, so bright it threatened to consume me.

A knock sounded lightly at the door. I stopped my pacing and gazed at it, my heart hammering and my mouth dry. Who could that be? Claire?

I answered the door. It was Gabe.

The sight of his face sent a rush of reassurance through me, and I leaned against the doorframe and shut my eyes briefly. I did not have the boldness to embrace him, but I smiled at him. Perhaps that was enough to convey my feelings.

"Hello," he said. His eyes were grave, almost unreadable. "You look pensive."

"I have much on my mind," I said, flicking my gaze over him. "You look pensive, too."

My whole body was a riot of nervousness and anxiety. The feelings were chewing me from the inside out. My eyes burned, but I didn't break down. I just breathed in the air, the scent of the forest and the wind. Gabe slipped his arms around me. "Tomorrow we go," he said. "We can deal with everything after that."

"Jacob wants to take everyone," I said.

"But what would you have him do? Leave them here? He can't do that."

I sighed, an admission of helplessness. "Sometimes there are no good answers, Gabe."

He didn't respond.

Finally, I untangled myself from the comfort of his arms. I needed sleep, although I wasn't sure if I'd find it tonight. "I'll see you tomorrow," I said, and he pressed his fingers against mine in promise.

When I reached the room, I was still in a snarl of anxiety. I paced until my feet hurt, and then I lay on the bed and rehearsed everything that must be done. My fingers itched to touch the device, to feel it safely in my hands. I rolled over and got on my hands and knees, digging under the bed for the place where I'd crammed the case against the spot between the bed frame and the wall. A secret hiding place, impossible to see unless you were looking for it.

But my fingers brushed empty air.

I bent down farther, half-crawling under the bed, reaching again.

Nothing.

"What—?" I muttered, fighting panic. I shoved the panel aside and looked.

The space was empty.

The PLD was gone.

~

I ran through the forest without stopping. The new necklace of snow blossoms I'd hastily thrown on bobbed around my neck with each stride, and my breath hissed as it left my lips. The Security Center was my only hope to find him tonight. I reached the doors, and they opened for me because I had clearance. A whoosh and I was down the tunnel and into the hall. My footsteps clanged, echoed. I stuck my head into every room, looking for him. Where could he be?

"Jacob? Jake?"

A few heads lifted, none of them the fugitive leader I sought. I darted down another hall. My heart pounded and my whole body surged with fear and fire. We were so close. How could this have happened?

A flicker of movement snagged my eye at the end of the hallway. *Jacob.* He was exiting the room where he'd originally spoken to me, the room where we'd originally talked about the PLD. How fitting. How ironic. I bit back the panicked urge to laugh.

"Lila?" He crossed his arms, waiting for me. Smirking?

"You bastard," I growled. "What do you hope to accomplish by these games?"

"What are you talking about?"

"Nobody knows how to work the device but me! You can't cut me out. You can't just take it and expect to—"

"Take it?" His face drained of color. "What...?"

"The PLD is gone," I spat. Why was he pretending not to know?

He put out a hand against the wall to steady him. *"What?"*

"Someone took it."

Jacob slammed his fist into the wall and swore loudly. I stared at him, taking in the reaction, and reality sunk in. "It wasn't you."

"Of course not," he snapped. "Why would I do that?'

"I..." To help the fugitives? I didn't finish my sentence. I just stared at him, trying to think. Of course he wouldn't. If he was fighting so hard to take everyone, did I really think he'd simply leave me?

Jacob scrubbed his hands through his hair and began to pace. "Who else knows about it? Think!"

Who else could have known about the PLD? Its existence had not been revealed to the other fugitives...no one except Gabe, but it couldn't have been Gabe. He was on the list. He was coming back with me...

My heart dropped like a stone.

Doctor Borde. He knew about the device, at least vaguely. It would have been easy for him to track down my room number, and search my room.

I'd been so foolish. I should never have trusted him, not even for information about the Sickness. And now, it was all falling apart. I sagged against the wall, trying to think, but my thoughts were slippery, loose, scattered. He might be in his private laboratory. I had to try, at least. "I—I have to go. Contact Gabe. Tell him to look everywhere he can think. I—I'll find you."

And before he could reply, I ran.

I had to get the device back tonight. If we didn't, the time window would close, and we'd be stuck here for another few weeks, at risk of exposure to the Sickness. Every day we remained here was that much more dangerous. Every day we remained here was another day Jonn, Ivy, and Everiss were without me.

What if we never got it back?

I refused to entertain that idea.

My heart pounded in time with my feet as I sprinted up the path and into the deeper forest, heading for Borde's private laboratory. Dark air swirled around me, hot and cloying, and sweat streamed down my back and soaked my hair. My side ached and my lungs burned, but I kept running.

Borde answered the door on the first knock. His hair was disheveled and his clothes dirty, as if I'd interrupted him in the middle of an experiment. At the sight of me, he opened his mouth as if to protest. I burst past him before he had time to invite me in or refuse me access.

"Give it back!" I demanded as soon as I'd reached the middle of the room. I scanned the shelves, the tables. I saw nothing resembling the PLD—but would he really be so foolish as to leave it lying out? He probably had it hidden away somewhere I'd never find it. I had to intimidate him. Threaten him. Something. I was desperate.

"You can't have it," he burst out, and fury took over my senses. I crossed the room in two strides and grabbed his arms.

"Give. It. Back."

His eyes widened until his pupils were just blue circles floating on a sea of white. "I—I cannot. It is mine. My research—"

"It is not yours. It belonged to my family."

"I found it—"

I let go of him. "Not your blasted journal, Borde. The PLD!"

"PLD?"

"The device. The device that's going to take me home, the one we talked about. It's gone. Don't play dumb. You must give it back, or...or I'll tell the other scientists about the journal. About your secret experiments. About what you gave me—"

He threw up his hands to quiet me. "Wait. Wait. The device has been stolen?"

I stopped, panting, as Borde stared at me with wide eyes.

"We need to make the jump tomorrow," I said.

"Oh no," he muttered.

TWENTY-TWO

"WHAT DO YOU know?" I demanded.

Instead of answering, Borde turned on his heel and disappeared through the doorway behind him in a flutter of shirtsleeves. I stood still for a second, my feet stuck to the floor and my head swimming with frustration and confusion, then I ran after him.

"Borde?"

No answer. Had he run away? Had he tricked me?

The hallway was dark as a cave, but I trailed my hands on the wall and followed the crack of light at the end. I entered a small room with a plain cot in one corner piled with rumpled sheets. Borde was rummaging in a closet. He yanked out a coat and a long, slender metal object. I took a step back, and he looked down at it and chuckled.

"It's a light," he said, clicking it on with his thumb. "I'm not going to hurt you."

I hovered in the doorway, not trusting him. Right now, I didn't trust anyone.

"Come on," he said. "We have to go now."

"Where are we going?"

"To find your device."

"How are you going to do that?"

"I think I know who might have taken it."

Instead of going out the front door, he led me down a flight of narrow steps and into an underground cavern. Lights snapped on, brilliant lights that hurt my eyes. A vehicle sat before us, glittering in the glare. Borde opened the door and climbed onto the seat. He motioned to the place beside him. "Get in. This will be faster."

Get into that thing? But there was no time to hesitate, no time to be afraid. No time to even think. My heart hammering, I grabbed the edge of the door and hoisted myself up, sliding into the seat he'd indicated. The vehicle smelled like leather and sweat. My throat tightened as Borde reached for the controls. He turned his wrist and I squeezed my eyes shut. There was a purr and a rumble beneath us. We lurched forward, and my eyes flew open again. The wall parted like a curtain and we were flying into the night.

Trees blurred past at a dizzying rate. We were moving faster than a horse at a gallop. My stomach churned as the vehicle tilted left and swerved right. Borde yanked the controls and mashed his hand on a control panel. Branches whipped against the sides of the vehicle and rocks flew past. I clung to the edges of my seat.

Finally, we ground to a stop outside the Labs.

"Quickly," Borde shouted, throwing open the door and clambering out. I scurried after him, stumbling as I landed on the ground at a run, and together we sped toward the doors to the Lab. Light shone from them, dim light because the hour was late. The only people here now were the night crew and the workers who cleaned, and perhaps a lone researcher or two working long hours.

The doors hissed quietly open, and cold air hit my face as we rushed inside. Borde seemed to know exactly where he was going. He hustled down a staircase without stopping to see if I was following. For an old man, he was shockingly spry.

We reached a long corridor on one of the lower levels. The lights here were dimmer, cooler. The walls were not so smooth, and the floors not so shiny. I'd never been this far down in the Labs, except in Frost time, with Adam. I remembered a room filled with books and overturned tables. The memory rushed past in a flash and was gone, just a tingle of a recollection of dust and Adam's cool eyes as we pounded down the hall. We skidded to a stop before a door. Borde threw it open, and we burst inside.

The room was empty. A plain desk and a chair greeted us. A single painting hung on the wall, the depiction of a set of mountains. Borde hissed something unintelligible beneath his breath and spun.

"We're too late," he said. "He's gone."

"Who's gone?"

Instead of replying, he ran back into the hall, and I had no choice but to follow again.

We returned to the night and the vehicle, which was purring where we'd left it. Borde climbed back in and barely waited for me to find a seat before we were off, whirling into the darkness and dodging trees and branches once more.

This time, we came to a stop outside the Security Center.

"Come on," Borde urged me. "I know what he's doing!"

We descended into the depths of the Center together and ran through the corridors, our footsteps echoing. The halls were empty. Every room we passed was devoid of security workers. The screens blinked and beeped unattended. When we reached the stairs, Borde threw out his hand to stop me. "Wait," he said. "Do you hear that?"

A faint clanging sound met my ears, like the blaring of a horn over and over. Borde jerked back and pressed his back against the wall.

"No," he breathed. "No no no. He didn't."

"He didn't what? What's going on?"

Borde shut his eyes and covered his mouth with one hand. "He activated them."

"What are you talking about?" I leaned over him, shaking him.

Borde blinked and focused on my face with the same piercing expression he'd looked at me with the first day he'd seen me in the Labs. "Listen to me and listen carefully," he said, grabbing me by both shoulders. "They turn away at the sign. It's how we designed them. Here—" He fumbled at his breast pocket and pulled out a card. I saw a flash of blue as he thrust it into my hand.

244

"Keep this with you, and if you show it to them, you'll be safe. Don't lose it, because I'm not sure if I'm right—"

"Right about what?"

But he was moving again, this time at a crouch. I dropped low and scuttled after him. I wasn't about to let him leave me behind.

As we moved down the hall, the blaring sound intensified.

"What is that sound?" I gasped. My ears throbbed as it grew louder.

"It's an alarm," Borde muttered. "Letting us know the security channels have been breached."

Ahead, I saw red lights flashing. My chest squeezed momentarily, a gut reaction to the scarlet glow, but it was simply bulbs in the wall. The blaring sound was emanating from a hole in the wall above the flashing lights, and when we reached the place below it, Borde yanked open a box on the wall and punched in a code. The sound cut off abruptly, and suddenly the hall was so quiet I could hear our harsh breathing in the stillness.

"Better," Borde muttered. "At least now I can hear myself think. Now come on, before he can get too far."

Who could get too far? We were at the Security Center—did he mean Jacob? But whose office had we gone to in the Labs? Where was everyone? What was that alarm?

But I didn't say anything this time, because I'd given up on asking questions of him. I simply followed as we reached a staircase and began to descend. Apprehension churned in my stomach and strung my muscles tight.

245

We reached a final, familiar hall. I recognized it from the night I'd first spoken to Jacob about the PLD. The sign at the end still proclaimed CAUTION: AUTHORIZED ENTRANCE ONLY.

But this time, like that first time, the door was open.

The darkness beyond gaped like a hungry maw, and Borde slowed as he approached it. He waved me back against the wall, and I pressed my shoulder blades to the cold stone. I watched as he crept forward and peered inside, and then he turned his head to look at me.

"Hurry," he breathed, and I joined him.

We slipped into the cavernous room, the one where Jacob and I had first discussed the PLD. I hadn't seen the interior of it before because everything had been dark, but now lights glittered like stars at the top of a lofty ceiling, faintly illuminating the room. My mouth fell open. Vast doors formed the far wall, and girders of steel crisscrossed the roof. Shelves formed a maze before us, a forest of metal. A swath of open floor stained with grease and dark patches of liquid lay between us and the doors. At the far end, I saw vehicles.

"He's here somewhere, I know it," Borde murmured. "Come on."

Faintly, at the edge of my awareness, I heard a clink.

Borde heard it, too. "This way," he said, and took off down one of the right-side rows. I followed at a run, focusing on keeping my footsteps as silent as possible.

Adam's training from before came flooding into my mind, giving me confidence. I moved smoothly, surely. I ran my gaze over the shelves, looking for ways to scale them if necessary, looking for any signs of threat just as he'd taught me to do. Ahead, Borde had reached the end of the row. He waited for me. When I joined him, he opened his mouth to speak.

The scuffle of an errant shoe came from the left. He froze, laid a hand on my arm, and lifted both eyebrows to signal that he'd heard it, too.

Ahead, in the shadows, I saw furtive movement. A figure clad in white slipped past us, heading for the vehicles and the massive doors in the wall.

Whoever it was, he was trying to escape.

Borde motioned for me to wait, and then he leaped out from his hiding place. "Gordon!" he shouted, and the word echoed all around us.

I looked. The figure stopped, turned. I sucked in my breath.

The dark-haired man, the one who had gazed at me so suspiciously. Doctor Gordon.

"Borde," he said, and his lips curled. "You found me."

"I knew you would run like a dog with his tail between his legs if you ever got your hands on the device, yes," Borde snarled. "But you aren't going to get away with this. You think I'm just going to let you steal all my research? Give me the device."

"Never. When I take it to the south and sell it as my own, then it will be my research, and if you try to claim otherwise, then you'll be the one who stole it," Gordon said. His gaze flicked to me, and he smirked. "No security guards?"

"They've all fled, just as you planned when you violated every security code we have—"

"Oh come," Gordon said with a low laugh, a chuckle that sent a chill trickling down my spine from the sheer malice of it. "Surely you're just as eager to see them in action as I am."

Borde was silent. His fingers twitched at his sides. He looked at Gordon's shoulder, and beneath the man's jacket I noticed the same thing Borde did—a long, straight bulge down the back. The device! He had it slung on his back, beneath his coat.

"The device...how did you even—"

"I saw you talking to her," Gordon said, jerking his head at me. "And I followed her to your private lab. I heard what she said about the device."

"But how did you steal it?" I burst out, unable to keep silent any longer.

"That little redhead was more than willing to tell me where your room was in exchange for something she needed."

I sucked in my breath. Claire had betrayed us?

"Give me the device," Borde repeated. He dug in his pocket and pulled out a box. "Or I'll call the Labs right now."

Gordon smiled and tipped his head to one side, ignoring Borde's threat. "Admit it. You aren't afraid of them; they won't attack you. Oh yes, I know about your little DNA failsafe."

What wouldn't attack him?

I looked from Borde to Gordon, but their faces gave me no indication of what they meant. Guards? The workers from the Security Center? And what failsafe was he talking about?

Gordon noticed my confusion, and his smile widened.

"She doesn't even know about them, does she? Otherwise she wouldn't dare be here."

"She is braver than you realize," Borde snapped. "And besides, she is not defenseless against them."

I remembered the card in my hand. I lowered my gaze and turned it over. It was white, with an image of a blue flower.

A snow blossom?

Dread knifed me in the gut. "Know what?" I asked, and my voice came out as just a whisper in the sudden silence.

The scrape of metal claws against stone made the hairs on the back of my neck rise. I turned so slowly, almost as if I were swimming in mud, as if my limbs had become paralyzed. A red gleam met my eyes, but it was not the lights from the hall.

It was the glow of eyes.

A Watcher.

TWENTY-THREE

I COULDN'T MOVE, couldn't speak, couldn't breathe.

There was a Watcher here, in this warehouse, in the Security Center.

And neither Gordon nor Borde seemed surprised by it.

The creature was medium-sized, larger than the vehicle we'd rode to the Security Center in, but smaller than any Watcher I'd see before. Spikes glittered along its back and down a lashing tail. The dog-like head turned to study me, and the massive clawed feet pawed at the ground. It looked like a giant cross between a cat, a wolf, and something else, something unholy and strange.

The blood-red eyes swept over me, casting light across the floor, and the Watcher snarled. Teeth gleamed in a gaping mouth, and the shoulders and haunches bunched as it launched toward me.

"Lia—" Borde began to shout, to warn me, but I was already moving as years of instinct kicked in. I dropped to the ground and rolled beneath the shelf, clutching the card to my chest.

Claws swiped at me, snagging my uniform and shredding the sleeve but narrowly missing breaking the skin. I thrust the card at the creature, remembering Borde's words, but the red wasn't reaching beneath the shelf to the darkness where I hid. The Watcher couldn't see the card I held, so the image wouldn't stop it from eviscerating me, not here.

I rolled away and hit a wall. I couldn't squeeze far enough away to be out of reach, so I began to crawl.

"Hey!" Borde shouted, attempting to draw the creature away. What was he doing? Was he mad, calling it to him instead of running?

The Watcher turned its attention from me to Borde and Gordon. Gordon smirked again and held up a sliver of metal that glimmered in the light. Borde clearly recognized it, whatever it was. I heard his sharp intake of breath.

"You idiot," he exclaimed. "Do you want to doom this whole Compound?"

"I wasn't the one who created them," the other man said.

Created them?

I reached the end of the shelves. If I could get across the row, I could climb up the other side and be out of reach. The Watcher was pacing toward Borde and Gordon, snarling. But the men didn't move. They stared at each other instead of the creature. I wanted to shout for Borde to watch out, but the words caught in my throat.

As I watched, Borde calmly withdrew a knife from his pocket and swiped it across his finger. A line of red appeared and ran down his arm. A single drop of blood splashed to the ground.

The creature stopped.

After an agonizing moment, it turned away from him and moved toward Gordon.

Confusion raced across my mind and sparked through my limbs. How had he turned the Watcher away? What had he done when he'd cut his hand?

But there was no time to think. I wriggled out from under the shelf and sprinted across the row to the other side. Grabbing hold of the support struts, I began to climb. My hands were sweaty, and they slipped on the metal rods that held the massive shelves aloft. I gritted my teeth and kept climbing. Behind me, I heard the snarls of the Watcher. When I reached the first shelf, I turned my head to see what was happening. Would the creature attack Gordon?

He lifted the hand that held the sliver of metal. The Watcher halted, its neck bent at an awkward angle and its claws raking the ground to gain purchase as it slipped. A grinding sound filled the air and the beast shuddered. It took a step back and swung around to look for me again, as if Gordon was invisible to it.

"With the controlling key, I can make it do whatever I want," Gordon said. "It's just a machine, after all."

Just a machine.

I didn't understand.

The Watcher whirled and spotted me. With a growl, it sprang in my direction. I scrambled higher, my lungs suddenly squeezed empty of air. The card slipped from my hand and fluttered to the floor like a fallen leaf. I swore. I swung one leg over the next shelf and hoisted myself up.

"Call him off," Borde shouted. "He'll kill her."

"Let me leave," Gordon responded smugly. "Or the girl dies."

Borde swung around to stare at me. Something flashed across his face, an emotion I couldn't name. The Watcher reached the bottom of the shelves and looked up at me. This one was limber, much more limber than the ones I'd seen in the Frost. Was it a young Watcher?

Gordon's words ran through my mind again, but I didn't have time to think about them. Not right now. I wriggled forward on the shelf, trying to gain enough of a foothold to climb to the next one. Below me, the Watcher paced. The long tail flicked. The eyes glowed.

"Gordon," Borde shouted again. "Stop it. Stop it now. This is murder!"

"Your move," the other man said. "Your decision. Throw me that communicator and let me leave, or I'll let it kill her."

The shelf shuddered behind me.

I turned in panic. The Watcher had leaped. It was right behind me. I felt the hot steam of its breath against my cheeks. The reds of its eyes burned into mine.

"Lia!" Borde called, ignoring Gordon. "Cut yourself! Make yourself bleed!"

The Watcher flashed its teeth at me.

I didn't hesitate. I dragged my finger across the broken edge of the shelf. Pain shot through my hand. Blood beaded on my skin.

Below, Borde watched intently, every line in his body strained. His hands clenched into fists, and his mouth worked as he muttered silent words.

"It won't work," Gordon said behind him, like the voice of a devil whispering to us. "Only members of your family can—"

The blood dripped down my fingers. Cold air rushed over my skin. The Watcher growled, and the sound rumbled in my bones. My legs shook. My lungs squeezed. My skin was hot, cold, slick with sweat and blood. I stood my ground and reached out.

The Watcher stopped.

It *stopped.*

"Oh," Borde gasped.

The head turned. The jaws closed. The eyes dimmed.

I sagged against the shelf supports in relief as the creature turned away and leaped down. It padded away into the darkness like a cat and was gone.

"Now," Borde said, his voice firm and full of triumph. "Give it to me."

He took a step toward Gordon. The other man flinched.

"Wait," he said. "You can't do this. I—"

"Give it to me, Gordon."

The dark-haired scientist hesitated a moment, then he turned and ran straight for the vehicles at the far wall.

Borde took off after him immediately, but he wasn't going to be fast enough to catch the younger man alone. "Lia," he shouted. "You've got to do something!"

I looked around wildly for something—anything—and my eyes fell on a large metal disc at the end of the shelf. A long shot, but worth trying. I grabbed it and scrambled down. My feet hit the floor and I was already sprinting down a side aisle, heading around to cut him off. I turned the corner and saw Gordon pass by. I darted after him. He left the maze of shelves and began to cross the vast expanse of open space that lay like a field between us and the doors at the other end of the room.

My lungs were fire and my blood ice as I closed the distance between us. To my right, Borde was running as fast as he could.

I hurled the metal disc at the back of Gordon's head. He howled in pain and fell, rolling as he clutched at the injury.

Borde reached him seconds after I did. I grabbed his hands as the older man wrestled him to the floor and yanked off the coat. He handed me the PLD case, and I tugged it open and almost fainted with relief when I saw the device nestled safely inside.

Gordon groaned from his place on the floor.

"Is it safe?" Borde panted, eyeing the device. His eyes burned with fascination, and I realized this was the first he'd seen of it.

"It's fine," I said. I ran my fingers over the gleaming metal as a surge of exhaustion flowed through me. "It's here and in one piece."

Borde reached out a hand as if he wanted to touch it. Gordon struggled, and he bent back over him, pinning him down. "Good throw," he muttered. "He's lucky you didn't kill him."

"What are we going to do about him? He knows too much."

Borde considered the problem. "We can...keep him out of the way until you are gone. I'll handle the rest."

I thought of Jacob. He could help us—if I dared to trust him. I wasn't sure that I did.

"We should get out of here," Borde said. He reached down and yanked the sliver of metal from Gordon's fingers, the one that had turned away the Watcher. "I need to call the rest of the Mechs off before they terrorize the whole compound. This idiot released them all so he could escape. Unlucky for him, I have a genetic override. They won't attack me."

"Mechs?"

"The creature," he explained.

The Watchers?

Now that I was not about to be eviscerated by a snarling monster, I remembered the things they'd said. Curiosity surged over me.

"Please—you must tell me everything."

Borde's mouth twisted in a smile. "Not here. Come on."

~

We returned to his private laboratory. Borde found a length of rope and bound Gordon's hands, and he tended to the cut on the back of his head before locking the scientist in the closet. He ordered me to sit and rest in one of the chairs while he made a few calls to the security team to explain how to deal with the other Watchers. Then he made tea. I balanced the PLD on my lap, waiting anxiously as thoughts ran circles in my head. Mechs, he'd called them.

The Watcher had turned away from Borde's blood.

It had turned away from mine, too.

When he returned, Borde also carried the journal. He set it on the table between us. An offer. Slowly, I did the same with the PLD. Perhaps it was time for a little trust on my part.

I watched as he lifted the device and cradled it like a baby. "It's magnificent," he said, his voice hushed with quiet wonder. "I...I made this, you see."

"What?"

"Yes. It is my design." He turned it over, deftly running his fingers over the buttons, the wires. "Incredible. So that's what I am missing..."

"If you made it..." I was confused. "How do you not know everything about it now?"

"I haven't made it yet," he explained. "But sometime in the future, I will." He paused. "I'm sure you have questions for me."

My mind was so full of thoughts and questions that I thought I would burst. "First, tell me about the creatures."

"What do you want to know about them?" he asked.

"Everything."

He drew in a deep breath and let it out slowly. "Where should I start?"

"You called them...Mechs?"

He nodded. "They are a new invention of mine. One of my finest."

"Invention? I don't understand. They are the ancient beasts that roam the Frost."

"The Frost?" Curiosity lit his eyes.

"This place is all covered in ice and snow in my time," I explained. "The Labs are a ruin called Echlos, and the creatures—we call them Watchers—guard it."

He exhaled. "So they still exist? They still perform their functions?"

I nodded. "But I don't understand. You...you made them?"

"They are machines," he said.

When I finally found my voice, I stuttered out my disbelief. "What? How is that possible? They are animals. They are intelligent, they are—"

"They are the most sophisticated artificial intelligence available," he explained. "Designed to learn and adapt. Nearly indestructible. They even...they can even make improvements to themselves. Grow, if you will. They are nearly self-sustaining, and they power themselves by sunlight. They prowl the night to protect the Compound."

"Why?" I asked.

He shook his head and rubbed his chin. "We've had too many threats since we began studying the Sickness, and the transport of animals has been restricted since the Sickness's spread. We needed higher security measures, and we had been working on a similar project for a client in the south. So, we built the creatures, a prototype. The Mechs. And they have exceeded my wildest expectations."

"In my world, we call them Watchers," I said. "We ward them off with snow blossoms."

"Ah," he said. "Real blossoms, you say?"

"Yes."

"Incredible. They must have learned to extrapolate from the symbol we use to repel them to the actual blossoms themselves," he breathed. "What magnificence. What brilliance..."

I didn't find the monsters who roamed my world killing and maiming quite as magnificent as he did, but I kept my opinions about his terrifying creations to myself.

Borde paused from his gushing about the Watchers' abilities and looked at me. "I want to know all about your world," he said, and eagerness shimmered in his voice.

"Wait. There's something else I must know. Something Gordon said." My chest tightened. "He said only you and your family could turn away the creatures with their blood."

Borde ran the tip of his finger across the journal. "It was a gamble. I have suspected, but I didn't know if I would be right. So when I told you to cut your finger, and the Watcher stopped at the scent of your blood..."

I held my breath.

He raised his head and looked me in the eyes. "It confirmed that you are my descendent."

The revelation went through me like a cold rush of sweet spring water. It was right, and yet it was strange, and yet...it was right. I nodded, taking it in with a lungful of air. Here, sitting across from me on a dusty chair, was my ancestor. The thought filled me with wonder, amazement. I reached out one hand, wanting to touch him, to make sure he was real, but I let my arm drop to the table instead. My eyes fell on the notebook sitting between us. I reached out and ran my fingers over the worn leather cover.

"And the journal? How did you get it? Where did it come from?"

"I found it years ago, as I said before. I saw it in a trash barrel and the design of the leather intrigued me. I quickly realized that whoever had written it had knowledge of the gate, of secrets that no one should know except me. But I don't know who wrote it, or why," he confessed. "But it quickly became apparent that whoever penned the journal knew of things I had not yet completed work on. And..." He hesitated. "It appeared to contain a sketch of my daughter, at least that's what I thought before I saw you." He thumbed the pages until he found the right one, and then he pushed the journal across the table to me. I stared. Shock shivered through me.

The sketch looked exactly like me.

That was why he'd stared, then. I remembered the intensity of it, the way his eyes had bored into me as if he was seeking to know every secret I hid.

"How...?"

"I don't know."

"Is that me?"

He shrugged. "When I saw you, I thought you might be connected to it somehow, but I could not be sure until I'd learned more. But when you knew the riddle written inside..." He broke off and stared at me, wide-eyed at the wonder of it.

"And you believe I am your descendent?"

"I'm sure of it. When I saw you, I had little doubt. You look so much like my wife, my daughter...it's remarkable. And then the incident with that Mech confirmed it."

"So my blood...the Watchers—Mechs, I mean—will not attack me if they can smell it?"

"They have sensors that read the information contained in it," he said with a nod. "You are forever safe to walk the forests of your world, Lia."

Wonder filled me. How long had my family harbored this secret in our veins? How long had we not known the power we possessed? And what would this mean for me once we returned? For Jonn and Ivy?

It meant we could walk the Frost unafraid. It meant we had something the Farthers did not. A smile stretched across my lips.

"Tell me about your world," Borde urged.

I hesitated as visions of the hushed forests of white filled my head. I saw the sky, so blue and lonely, ringed by mountains and punctuated by storm clouds. I saw the path lined with snow blossoms, the color of hope and fear. I smelled the scent of pine and melting ice and tasted the chill of the wind.

"It is so beautiful and so deadly," I said. "All of this is gone, almost. The town remains and it is my village. We have none of your technology anymore. The Watchers are drawn to it. They attack."

He lowered his head a little. "They are your enemies now?"

"We are afraid of them," I said. "But also they keep us safe. It is a precarious balance. A dance of life and death."

"And the Sickness? Have you found a cure in the future?" he asked.

I shook my head. "We have no Sickness in the Frost." I thought about Adam and my heart twisted painfully. "It still exists in the coastal regions. Some have fled to our lands to escape it."

"Fascinating," Borde murmured. "And you say you have renounced technology completely?"

"We live very primitively compared to you," I said, gesturing at the lights that glowed in his ceiling, and at the door that hissed open and shut at the touch of a button. "We have horses, wagons, lanterns."

"Such a change from the way things are now," he mused.

"Yes."

We sat in silence a moment, and then he pushed the journal toward me.

"I think perhaps you should finally see this."

I lifted the book carefully, my blood humming in anticipation. I turned to the first page and gasped at the image scrawled there.

A broken Y.

The sign of the Thorns.

TWENTY-FOUR

"DO YOU KNOW what this symbol means?" I demanded, showing the drawing of the Thorns emblem to him. Shock and surprise pulsed through me. My skin prickled and my hair rose as I looked from his face to the sketch on the page in front of me.

But Borde shook his head, his expression blank, his eyebrows pinched together in curiosity. "No. Does it mean something to you?"

"Yes." I left it at that and turned the page, my head swimming with astonishment. An almost unintelligible scrawl filled the pages, mostly strings of words that made no sense to me. Numbers. Colors.

"Much of the book is utter nonsense to me," Borde said. "I don't know what it means. What else do you recognize?"

I turned another page and sucked in a breath. Here it was.

What woven secret will keep you warm?

I traced the words with my fingertip. "It was my father's riddle," I said. "And the answer led us to the PLD." I tapped my hand against the device. "The woven secret was my mother's quilt—a map of the Frost—and we found the hiding place of the device hidden in the stitches." I turned another page and saw another word that made me dizzy.

Weavers.

"My family name," I said.

Borde's eyes were alight with interest, but I glanced at the clock and my heart sank.

"I have to get back and find my friends. They will be frantic. We're out of time. And I can't tell them about you."

"I understand," he said. He gathered up the teacups and rose to carry them to the kitchen. When he returned, he looked at the PLD but didn't touch it.

"Before," he said. "You said you are all leaving tomorrow. Or, today, rather." He glanced at the clock ruefully.

"Yes," I said. "We have to make the jump back during the window of opportunity, and that only comes at certain specific intervals. And we don't dare stay longer with the Sickness spreading."

He nodded, absorbing this. I could tell he had more questions that he longed to ask, but he was restraining himself. I was grateful. I didn't know how much I could answer, or how much I should reveal. I'd already told him far too much...but so had he.

The weight of the secrets I'd accumulated pressed against me as I rose from the chair and picked up the PLD. I snapped the case shut and slung it over my back.

"Come," Borde said. "I'll drive you back."

~

I climbed from his vehicle at the entrance to the town. I didn't want anyone to see me with one of the top scientists of the Compound and start asking questions. I made the rest of the trek in the dark, and when I reached the barracks, I went inside and trudged to my room. Every muscle in my body screamed with exhaustion, but I didn't know if I even had time to catch more than a few hours of sleep. Also, I needed to find Jacob somehow and let him know that I'd found it.

When I stepped inside my room, hands grabbed me.

"Gabe," I gasped, relieved when I recognized him.

"What's going on?" he demanded. "Jacob is frantic. He says the PLD is missing. There's a security breach at the Center. Everyone is on lockdown—"

"I've got it," I interrupted. "I found it." I slung the device off my shoulder and set it on the bed.

"What? How—?" He looked from my face to the PLD as his shoulders sagged with relief.

"It is an impossibly long story," I said. "Do you think you can find Jacob and tell him? He wasn't at the Security Center."

"When were you at the Security Center?"

"Not long ago." I fingered the dried blood on the place where I'd cut my finger.

"No one is supposed to go there now. There's been a breach."

"I know," I admitted, the sentence an exhale. I sank onto the bed beside the device. I felt scraped, squeezed, and strung too thin.

Gabe studied my expression for a moment. "You have things you aren't telling me," he said finally.

"I'm sorry." It was all I could offer, at least for now.

He nodded. I couldn't tell if he was angry or not. "I will find Jacob and bring him here to speak with you."

"Thank you."

He pressed a hand to my cheek, and then he went out and I was alone.

I locked the door, tumbled into the bed, and shut my eyes.

But sleep wouldn't come. Thoughts filled my head. Ideas.

Atticus had told me only to bring the people on the list. In fact, he'd threatened my family if I didn't. However, the situation here was becoming increasingly dangerous. I couldn't just leave them. What about Juniper, Claire, the children...Gabe? With the Sickness spreading and the threat of war, I didn't have the heart to deny anyone passage home, but my loyalty lay first with my family.

I touched the dried blood at the end of my finger, thoughtful. My mind spun. I was a Weaver. My blood gave me access to the Frost in a way no one else's did. And...the same was true for Jonn and Ivy.

It was my trump card.

Atticus wouldn't dare hurt them. Not if they were worth so much. I had to count on that.

When the footsteps finally signaled Gabe's return, I had washed and dressed in a clean uniform. My eyes felt full of sand and my muscles still ached, but I felt alert again. I was ready.

It was time.

Gabe knocked and I let him in. Jacob stood behind him, eying me warily. They stepped inside and shut the door. "You've got it back?"

"Yes, no thanks to Claire."

"Claire?" Gabe interrupted. "What does she have to do with it?"

"She helped one of the scientists steal the PLD."

"I don't believe it," he said.

"It's true." I crossed my arms and glared at them both, daring them to argue further.

Jacob scowled. "I'll tell the others to watch for her, but there's little we can do about that at the moment. We have to get out of here. What about the matter of the list?"

There was much that needed to be said, as much as I didn't want to deal with this now. I looked from him to the PLD.

"You don't want to leave anyone behind—"

"I won't." He gritted it through clenched teeth.

"I know," I said. My stomach twisted into a knot of apprehension. This was the move I'd decided was the best one. The smartest one. It was the gamble that just might pay off. "So...we'll take them all."

Gabe straightened, blinked.

Jacob's eyebrows lifted in surprise. "Just like that?" he asked.

"Just like that." I crossed my arms, hiding my cut finger.

"What's the catch?" he asked. Suspicion leaked into his tone. He looked at the PLD again.

"No catch," I assured him. "But you have to know...you go to a difficult situation. Aeralian soldiers have occupied my village, led by an officer called Raine. There is little food, and the Frost is, as you may know, quite dangerous."

"I know," he said. "But right now I think it's safer than staying here."

~

The fugitives gathered in the meeting room in the basement where they had their weekly meetings. Someone had spread the word—I didn't know who. By the time Jacob, Gabe, and I arrived, they had all assembled. Tired faces and expectant eyes turned toward us as we entered the room. I looked, but didn't see Claire.

Did she know we were looking for her? Did she know we knew what she'd done?

I stopped at the back of the room. The PLD thumped against my shoulder blade as I toyed with the case strap. I set down my bag of clothes and other things, which now included the mysterious sealed box from Borde that

I was bringing back for Jonn. Gabe stood beside me and his presence gave me strength.

Jacob stepped to the front of the room and addressed the fugitives.

"Fellow travelers," he said. "Today, we are offered a choice. A chance. A gift. We have a way to return home to the world we came from, to the life we left."

"But what do we return to?" someone called. "We've built a life here for ourselves."

"Yes, but the Sickness—" another began.

Jacob lifted his hands, calling for quiet. The questions died away to a low murmur, an undercurrent that punctuated his next words. "Nobody has to go if they don't want to," he said. "We will be returning to perilous times. The device—a type of gate—returns us to the Frost at the exact place where we originally left. Aeralian soldiers now occupy it. There is little food or shelter for us. It will be hard. I will not pretend otherwise. However, I want everyone who wishes to return to have the opportunity. This world will not be safe forever."

He meant the Sickness, we knew, and other things. Everyone knew that this world no longer existed in the future. What nobody knew was when it ended. Nobody knew how long it would be safe to stay.

Silence swept the room. Heads turned, wide eyes met and held. I could see them evaluating. If they left now, would they be leaping from the frying pan into the fire?

My gaze fell on two small children sitting beside a woman in a gray uniform, and my heart stuttered as I recognized them. The two fugitive children I'd rescued in the forest and hidden in my barn. The boy gazed at me with solemn eyes, giving no sign that he recognized me, and the girl stared at the ground. Their chests rose and fell with even breaths. The woman sitting beside them patted the boy's shoulders, and I wondered if they wanted to come back to the harsh, unforgiving world they had left. This one must have been kinder to them.

Suddenly, the urge to speak was almost more than I could bear. I cleared my throat and spoke loudly, so my voice would carry over the whispered words.

"Fellow fugitives," I said.

Heads swiveled in my direction. I licked my lips, apprehensive. My hands were clammy and my legs trembled, but I had no time to focus on fear. I needed to speak my piece.

"I don't want anyone to be deceived. As Jacob said, if you come back with us, you return to perilous times. There is little food. Never-ending snow. Watchers. The Aerialian soldiers have taken over my village. Our world is unsafe." I paused. "But it is our world. Our families are there." I thought of Ivy, of Jonn. "Those we love are there." Adam flashed before my eyes, and I blinked. Ann too. I pushed away those thoughts. I did not have time for them, not right now. "So I won't pretend it will be easy. Here you have warmth and food and some veneer of safety. There is the Sickness, yes. There is talk of war, yes. But in many ways it is easier. So, you choose, but if you return with us, you are going to have to hide again. You are going to have to struggle. You are going to have to take an oath of loyalty—" I paused again and looked at Jacob firmly. "—to the Thorns."

I checked the faces of the travelers. They were listening. I saw Juniper at the back of the crowd, watching me intently.

He was nodding.

Strength flowed through me in a surge, and I lifted my chin and spoke louder, clearer. "If you come back with us, you will bind yourselves to secrecy. You will join with us, swear loyalty to our cause. You have seen much and your knowledge is dangerous. But you can help. You can make a difference."

Their expressions were ragged with hope and fear and uncertainty. Eyes softened at my words and mouths curved. I could see that they were tired. They were tired of waiting, doing nothing, simply existing like rats in a hole. I could see that my words were feeding strength and courage into hearts.

"So come," I said. "And join us. Or stay. Only commit to do what you know you can. Commit what you know you can keep."

With that, I knelt to the ground and began to take out the device from its case.

It was time to go.

Gabe crouched beside me. "What can I do?" he asked. "I want to help."

The PLD was heavy in my hands as I placed it on the ground. My fingers tingled against the cold metal, and as

I powered it on, light glittered over our faces and danced on his face. Our eyes met and held. A world of unspoken things passed between us. Vulnerability, empathy, hope.

I withdrew the page with Jonn's scribbled instructions from my pocket and passed it to him. "Help me," I said, and my words were an invitation of trust.

Jacob was speaking again. "If you wish to go, gather your things and return in less than half an hour. If you wish to stay, say your goodbyes."

The people rose and began reaching for one another. Mouths moved, hands squeezed hands.

Gabe helped me lay out the wires and punch in the codes. The PLD hummed to life beneath our fingers. Green light shot out in streams and played across the ceiling of the room, making patterns like light over water. Light leaked from the seams. Once I'd arranged the wires in the right pattern—each one stretched out straight at equal distances from the others, like spokes splaying from a wheel—I pressed the largest button, and the PLD sprang to life.

Light erupted from the center in a column that plumed outward, fanning into a circle of pulsating energy. A low rumble filled the room. Jacob went very still as he stared at the newly made gate.

"Incredible," he whispered, and wonder leaked into his voice.

The light danced and snaked in lazy spirals in the center of the gate's eye. I was transfixed as I watched the colors collapse and reanimate. It was like strange fire, like the lights that sometimes danced in the winter sky. It was beautiful.

Gabe's fingers found mine. "We've each done this alone," he said, "but this time we're going to do it together. Don't be afraid."

"I'm not," I said out of habit, because I was always the strong one whether it was true or not. But then, I realized that the words I spoke were true. I wasn't afraid. I was full of wonder, exhilaration. Happiness.

I was going home.

The door opened, and Juniper re-entered the room. I hadn't even seen him leave. He carried two packs with him. "If you're going to be living in a place with not much food, you might need some supplies," he said with a weary laugh. He dropped the packs at our feet. "This should feed a few people for a week."

I bent and opened one of the packs. Cans of food glittered in the green light of the gate. I raised my eyes to his. "Thank you," I said.

He nodded somberly.

I found Jacob. "If the others do not return in time, they will be left," I said.

"I understand."

Agitation rippled through my blood as the minutes ticked past. I itched to turn and step through that gate, but we had to wait. According to Jonn's instructions, once we opened it, we would only have a little time. We had to wait and all go at once.

The door creaked open and shut as some of the fugitives returned. I counted more than a dozen that gathered around us, clutching packs and bags and wearing their coats. The two young children who I'd personally rescued months before were among those preparing to leave. Their eyes were round and their mouths clamped tightly shut. They clung to each other, but they didn't cry. The thin woman was not with them.

I wondered what thoughts ran through their young minds. How did one make such a decision at such an age?

"Is everyone assembled?" Jacob asked. He swept the crowd with his gaze as the travelers muttered and looked around. It was less than a third of the fugitives.

I checked the clock. We had five more minutes until we left.

A few more people trickled in and joined us.

And then, it was time.

I activated the gate. The light peeled back like the widening of a pupil in the middle of a vibrant green eye. The blackness in the middle writhed and breathed.

I pointed at Jacob. "Go."

He sucked in a breath, lifted a pack to his shoulders, and stepped into the space. And he was gone.

One by one, the travelers followed. And one by one they vanished, until only Gabe and I were left. We looked at each other.

"You first," I said, and he nodded.

When he vanished, tears flooded my eyes. It was the same and yet it was so wholly different. I dragged in a final lungful of the hot, moist air of this younger place and prepared to step forward.

The door banged behind me. Claire burst into the room, and her eyes widened as she saw the vortex. She darted past me and through the gate before I could stop her.

The door opened again, and Doctor Borde stumbled into the room. His mouth dropped open in wonder at the glow of the gate. "Wait—Lia!"

I had no time. The gate was closing.

His face was the last thing I saw before the darkness took me.

TWENTY-FIVE

BLACKNESS FADED TO gray, and the gray bleached to white. A rushing filled my ears. My limbs tingled. I was cold.

So cold.

Hands found mine and squeezed. Pain lanced my eyes as I tried to open them. A tremble shot through my limbs, and I rolled over and coughed. My hands scrabbled across something slick and hard and cold. Dampness seeped through my knees. Ice.

"Lia." It was Gabe's voice.

He helped me stand. I cracked open my eyelids against the light and sucked in a ragged breath. The air was so cold and dry that it burned my lungs.

"We made it."

I opened my eyes.

The gate stretched above us, cold and impotent, sleeping. Travelers lay scattered across the room in various poses of lying, sitting, and crouching. A few people had vomited. Some were moaning. I spotted Juniper climbing to his feet. He hissed through his teeth and shook his head.

"I'd forgotten how much I hate that trip," he muttered, wiping sweat from his face with one hand.

"Claire..." I growled, and Gabe shook his head.

"She went that way." He pointed at one of the dark holes that led into the depths of lower Echlos.

I scrubbed both hands over my eyes and sighed. I had far more to worry about right now besides that traitor.

Gabe helped me limp across the room to where Jacob sat with his back to the wall and his head in his heads. He groaned and lifted it as I reached him. "What now?" he asked.

I glanced around the room. "I need to get you to Atticus soon. He needs to speak with you at once."

"And them?" Jacob gestured at the fugitives.

I ran my eye over the group, counting them. Almost twenty people. We could never house them all at the farm or at Adam's property. They could not go to the village, of course, not all of them, and certainly not all at once. If we wanted to try to integrate them, it would have to happen slowly so as not to attract Raine's—or Korr's—attention.

Korr. Gabe. I inhaled sharply as I realized that could be a potentially difficult situation. What if someone saw Gabe and recognized the resemblance? What would Korr do if he found out Gabe was here in the Frost again?

We needed a secure place to hide.

I remembered. Some of the lower rooms, in the lower levels—they were warmer, more sheltered than this one.

It was so simple and so brilliant.

"We'll stay here for now," I said. "There are lower levels that provide more shelter."

"Here?" Gabe said sharply. "But the Watchers—"

The Watchers. He was right. I shut my eyes. I was safe as a Weaver, as a descendent of Borde, and so was my family. But the rest of these people...

We'd have to be careful.

~

I left the fugitives in the room where Adam and I had first discovered papers about the PLD and then I plunged into the woods surrounding Echlos with Jacob at my side and the sack of my things in my hand. The snow crunched beneath my feet. The air made my cheeks numb and my mouth ache as I breathed, but I relished the icy wind on my tongue. It tasted like home.

We wove around rocks and past frozen streams beginning to thaw. Through breaks in the foliage above our heads, I could see the beginning of a storm brewing. Good. The snow would cover any tracks we left today. Jacob said nothing, but he kept up with my pace and didn't falter even when a pack of mothkats rushed up from a rotted stump as we passed.

Finally, we reached my home. I stepped through the branches and into the clearing. A tendril of smoke curled from the chimney and light glowed in the windows. A knot in my chest eased. I exhaled and started forward.

"Is this where we'll find Atticus?" Jacob asked, following. He looked from my face to my family's farm.

"Soon," I promised. "But I just have to do one thing first. Wait in the barn and I'll join you again in a few minutes."

I ran for the house. The Watcher Ward clanged above my head as I wrenched open the door, and then Jonn and Ivy and Everiss were staring up, startled, as I stumbled inside.

"Lia!"

Ivy almost knocked me over with her hug before Jonn reached me, wheezing and limping on his crutches. He almost fell into my arms, and he wrapped both arms tight around my neck and buried his face in my shoulder. Everiss hovered a safe distance away, but her eyes gleamed with relief.

"There's no time," I breathed finally, smoothing my siblings' hair with my hands as I relished their warmth, their solidness. Hugging them had convinced me that they were real, that they were whole, and that they were truly alive and safe. That was all I'd needed before facing Atticus. "I have one more thing to do now before the mission is finished. I just had to make sure you were safe."

"We are well," Jonn assured me, lurching back a little and leaning heavily against the table. "I'm just so glad to see you alive."

I hugged him again. "I found Borde. I brought what you asked," I whispered in his ear, and he pulled back and stared in my face.

I handed him my sack of things without saying anything else. Wordlessly, he reached in and found the sealed box from Borde. A vein in his throat pulsed as he gazed at it.

I wanted to ask him what it was, but I had other things to worry about now.

"I must go," I said, although the words filled me with an ache. "I have a friend waiting. But—" My stomach tightened, but regardless of the mixed emotions I felt, I had to ask. "Have Adam or Ann been here lately? Have they returned? I want to know that they are safe, too."

"Oh," Ivy said, and when Jonn shot her an angry look she turned red.

"What?" I demanded.

Jonn sighed and rubbed a hand over his face. "Finish your mission, Lia. Then we can talk."

"No," I said. "Let's talk now. What is it?"

He scowled but knew better than to argue. "Ann is...in Aeralis."

"I know," I said. "She hasn't returned?"

"She is there indefinitely," he said.

My stomach fell. My mind spiraled. I stared at him. "Indefinitely?"

"Yes...Thorns business, I've been told." He cut a glance away and then raised his eyes back to mine. "Adam, too."

I couldn't breathe.

They were gone? Forever?

"Are you sure? How do you know?"

"Atticus told us."

Atticus. I had kept that secret from them. What had happened in my absence? "How do you know him?"

Jonn and Ivy looked at each other. Jonn opened his mouth to speak.

"Wait. Didn't you say you had someone waiting in the barn?" Everiss interrupted.

We all turned to look at her.

"Atticus is in the barn," she said. "Waiting for Lia. He said he expected her back."

"What?" I shouted.

~

I yanked open the barn door. "Atticus!"

The shadows shifted and I saw them both. Jacob's expression was unreadable. Atticus's was pleased. I decided he must not yet know about the fugitives that had returned with us.

"Lia Weaver," he greeted me. "You were successful, I see."

"Why did you involve my siblings in this? I wanted them kept out of it!"

"My dear," he said. "I am rapidly running out of agents. With you gone through the gate, and Adam and the Mayor's daughter otherwise occupied, I had no choice."

"Jonn said Ann and Adam have gone to Aeralis indefinitely," I spat. "On *your orders.* How can you say you had no choice?"

"They have gone away and I don't know if or when either will return," he drawled. "But I had nothing to do with it. Your former leader has gotten himself captured by the enemy while he was on a mission for the Thorns that he involved himself in independently of me, against my orders I might add, and he is currently on his way to a prison cell. And your friend has been summoned under suspicion of involvement with enemy combatants. She aroused the notice of that man Korr. But she's making the most of an unfortunate situation by gathering information for us."

Shock sizzled through me, but I fought to keep my mind clear of it. Captured? Summoned under suspicion of involvement with... "Enemy combatants?" I demanded.

"Adam Brewer," he said. "And...you."

My eyebrows shot up.

"I'm here to warn you, actually," he said. "Don't go into the village. They think you've fled, you know. They know you aren't here, but you can't come back."

"What?" Blood rushed to my ears. A hole of dread opened beneath my boots, and I was falling hard as I stared at his emotionless face and absorbed what he was telling me.

"Gather your things," he continued. "I heard just an hour ago that Raine is sending soldiers to confiscate this farm, and I came to warn your siblings. There is little time. You will have to run."

"Where?" But my mind was already working. Echlos. We could run to Echlos. Our blood would keep us safe. It was our secret. The Weaver's secret.

"Hurry, girl," Atticus snapped, and I whirled and ran for the house.

TWENTY-SIX

"I CAN'T GO with you," Ivy blurted out after I'd delivered the news.

"What are you talking about?" I stared at her, aghast.

"I can't go with you. I have to stay here."

"Didn't you hear what I said?" I wanted to shake her. "Soldiers are coming. They might already be on their way. We have to go now."

"I know," she said. "I will stay here and let them find me. I can say Jonn ran away, too. I'm just a child in their eyes, so they'll reassign me to a new family. They won't lock me up. I'm in the school. As far as they know, I'm already in their clutches."

"You can't be serious."

"She makes a good point," Atticus interjected.

I shot him a murderous look. "I'm not leaving my baby sister for Raine's soldiers to arrest. I won't leave her behind."

"Lia," Ivy said. She put her hand on my arm. "I'll be all right. I can do this."

"No." I looked to my twin brother for support, but he was gazing at the ground as if deep in thought. His

lips were pressed in a firm line, and a wrinkle formed between his eyebrows.

"Listen to me, Lia," Ivy said. "I already have a place in the town. I attend the Farther school now, and they think I'm turning into a perfect little model Farther citizen. When they reassign me to a foster family after you're gone, I can begin learning another trade. I'll be in a perfect position to help the Thorns. I can sneak out to visit you and bring you some of the food I earn from attending the school. And I can help you! They'll believe me when I tell them I'm not with the Thorns. They won't arrest me...I'm just a child to them. They might watch me closely, but I'm already enrolled in their school. They won't torture me or lock me up."

I gazed at her, amazed. She stood confident, firm, tall, and my heart tore into pieces as I looked at her and knew that she spoke sense. I wanted her to run to the uncertainty of a broken ruin and a cold, wintery forest populated by monsters. What was wrong with me?

"I have to pack," I managed to say, and I fled to my parents' bedroom.

Jonn hobbled in a few minutes later to find me wrapping up pots and pans in some of my mother's quilts and tying them shut with rope.

"Lia," he said, gently.

I shook my head and kept working.

He sank on the bed beside me, and I leaned into him and put my face in his shoulder just as he'd once done with me. Had that been only two weeks ago? It felt like years.

"How can we leave her behind?" I gasped, my voice muffled.

"She isn't a little girl anymore," he said, stroking my hair. "She's growing up. And she's right. It makes more sense for her to stay. They won't arrest her, and she can continue attending the school and earning food. She'll be safer here than in the forest, where everything is so uncertain, so dangerous. The Watchers—"

"We don't have to be afraid of Watchers anymore, Jonn."

He was silent. "You know things," he said finally. "You learned them there, I can tell. What is it?"

"There's...there's too much. There's not enough time. We have to hurry." I drew back and rubbed my forehead. "You are right. She is right. This is the safest option for her. And...the best option for the Thorns."

Jonn grinned ruefully. "You can't keep her from it forever."

"I know."

"But if things get dangerous, she can leave and come with us. We won't be too far. Will we?"

"Yes," he agreed. "We won't be too far."

~

We took the horses with us, along with everything we could carry or stuff into bags. My mother's quilts. Extra sets of clothing. Pots and pans, books, socks, our remaining bags of precious grain. The chickens, the cow, soap, mirrors, and combs. Everything we could carry or load on the animals, we brought, because we'd need all these things and more if we were going to live in the Echlos ruins. Jacob and Atticus helped, carrying what they could from the house to the tethered horses. Jacob was the one who lifted Jonn in his arms and helped him climb astride the gelding.

Finally, we were ready.

Ivy stood in the yard, brave and dry-eyed, watching us prepare to go. She wrapped her arms around her midsection as if she was holding herself together, but when I hugged her tight she was the one who rubbed my back in small circles as if reassuring me. I wondered in astonishment at the change in her.

"I'll be fine," she whispered, and then she pushed me away. My whole body ached with sadness, but there wasn't time to think. We ran, heading toward the trees in different directions, leaving multiple sets of footprints so the soldiers wouldn't know which to follow. Ivy was running behind us, muddling them, crisscrossing the yard with as many footprints as she could make. Her smile flashed and she waved, and then we were plunging into the Frost and she slipped from sight.

I could barely breathe, but I kept walking, because I was a Weaver, and Weavers kept going no matter what.

The Frost was just a blur of white around us as we fled. Jacob and Atticus kept pace beside me, and Jonn and Everiss joined us as soon as they'd left tracks in the opposite direction and backtracked along one of the deer trails. We meet in a clearing ringed with snow blossoms.

"Where do we go now?" Everiss asked. Her eyes were wide as she stared at the darkening forest around her. Her breath escaped her lips in a tendril of white, and it look like a ghost.

"Echlos," I said. "It's the only place that's safe now."

"No," Atticus said.

I swung around to face him. He stood still, feet planted wide, his cloak swirling in the wind and flecks of snow blowing past his cheeks.

"What do you mean, no?"

"You cannot take them there."

"We have to. There isn't much time—"

"The other fugitives are there," Jacob added. "We can't leave them alone for long. They'll need direction for settling in and keeping safe for the night, at least in that ruin. They'll need food and warmth, especially the children."

"Children?" Atticus's gaze sharpened. He looked at me. "There were no children on my list, Weaver."

"We couldn't leave them," Jacob interjected, dragging the attention from me. "Not with the Sickness, sir. *I* couldn't leave them. Anyone who comes under my care is family to me, and I don't let anything happen to my family. We made a judgment call based on the circumstances, and I think it was the right one."

"I see," Atticus said shortly. He folded his hands and said no more.

My heart thudded. I knew it would not be so simple. Someone would pay for this later. Probably me.

I didn't have time to worry about that now, though. We had to get to safety before night fell and the Watchers came out. Before Farther soldiers found us. Before we froze in the gathering storm.

We were vulnerable, and there were any number of ways that we could die.

"Let's keep going," I said.

We pressed on into the bluish haze of the twilight. Bits of ice sliced my cheeks and the backs of my hands. Behind me, Jonn and Everiss clung together on the back of the horse, their eyes dull with exhaustion and cold. Neither one of them was accustomed to the cold like I was, with my frequent forays into the Frost. Jacob struggled through the snowdrifts at the very back, and Atticus stalked beside me. His expression was unreadable, but I knew he was angry.

Finally, we reached the hill just before the plain that held Echlos. Relief spread its wings in my chest, and I surged forward with a final burst of strength. "We're here. Hurry—we need to get inside before the—"

"Not so fast."

The edge in Atticus's voice pulled me up tight. I stopped, turned.

He stood closest to me. His black cloak curled in the wind, fluttering around him. His shoulders were rigid. "We need to talk about what we're going to do about the extra fugitives you brought back against my orders."

"Listen, Atticus—"

"I've already figured out a way to rectify your mistake," he said sharply. "You will go inside and ask everyone who wasn't on the list to follow you. You will lead them to the village and abandon them where the soldiers can find them. Raine will think he's captured the rest of the Thorns operatives—"

"What? That's a terrible idea," I argued. "I'm not letting them get arrested. We aren't sacrificing them to save our own necks. I'm sorry about the extra people, but we'll make do. They could be useful to us. Besides, if Raine gets hold of them, he'll only interrogate them and learn about Echlos. Is that what you want?"

"He can't interrogate them if they're dead."

"No," I said firmly. A prickle of horror slid down my spine. As the fabric slipped away from his arms, I saw the weapon in his hands. My father's gun.

"What are you doing?" The words tore themselves from my throat and floated on the wind as Atticus took a step closer to me.

"Agents must do as they're told," he growled. "If you won't follow my orders willingly, then you'll have to obey them with a gun in your face."

"Are you crazy?" I demanded. My tongue stuck to my teeth. My hands trembled. "That weapon will attract Watchers!"

His finger tightened on the trigger, his eyes squeezed into a squint. "I'm tired of your excuses and lies."

"Stop!" Jacob shouted.

He moved before anyone else had time to blink. He yanked Atticus against him and pressed a blade to the man's back. "Drop your weapon."

"What is this?" Atticus hissed. "What are you doing?"

"All those who came through the gate are part of my family...and I don't let anything happen to my family," Jacob growled. He pressed the knife into the folds of fabric of Atticus's cloak, and the other man winced. "Now drop your weapon."

Atticus elbowed him in the face and whirled toward me. Jacob clutched his bleeding face and clawed at Atticus's arm. The gun went off.

The sound ripped the air open. I fell back, my ears ringing. The horses reared on their hind legs, snorting. Jonn's mouth was moving. He was shouting at me, but I couldn't hear what he said. I scrambled to my feet. My hands stung from the ice, and my hair fell into my eyes. I saw Jacob and Atticus struggling. The knife flashed in Jacob's hand, and Atticus wrenched away and took aim at me again.

The roar filled the air like thunder.

Everyone froze.

Watchers.

Atticus spun in a circle, aiming at the trees. His eyes searched the shadows.

"Your weapon will do nothing," I called. "It will only attract them to you."

Jacob took a nervous step back. "Lia?"

"We need to get inside," I said. My mind spun. In the past, my blood had turned away the creatures. Would they still recognize the signal that caused them to turn

292

away, or had that knowledge faded over the last 500 years?

The first beast stepped from the trees. It was a massive one, twice the size of the Watcher I'd confronted in the Security Center. Massive eyes glowed the color of scarlet. The long, wolfish head turned to look at us, and the jaws cracked open. Teeth sparkled like knifes.

Knives... I needed a knife to cut my hand.

Another Watcher emerged from the trees, a smaller and more agile one than the first. Its eyes glowed as it paced toward us. The horses whinnied nervously and tossed their heads.

"Don't move," Atticus snarled, pointing the weapon at me. "Don't you dare run, Lia Weaver."

I froze, staring down the barrel.

"Atticus..."

He fired the gun, but then Jacob was there, pushing me out of the way, his body jerking as the bullet struck him. I fell into the snow on my hands and knees. "Jacob!" I shouted, but he lay still, unmoving.

The first Watcher launched forward, snapping at Atticus. He shot at it, and the bullet clanged harmlessly off the Watcher's shoulder with a flash of sparks. The scaly skin tore, and through the gap I saw the flash of something metallic. The Watcher threw back its head and screamed. Only one thought filled my head—knife. Jacob had dropped it. But where?

I threw myself down into the snow, searching for it as Atticus fired another shot at the beast.

The second Watcher ran at Jonn and Everiss with a guttural snarl. I heard Everiss scream.

"Jonn! Cut your finger and then ride for Echlos as hard as you can!"

I didn't look to see if he did as I'd asked. My fingers touched cold steel. I pulled the blade across my middle finger, and red sprouted along the tip. Dimly, I heard Atticus shriek in pain and become abruptly silent. Hot breath hissed over my shoulders, red glowed all around me, and I raised my hand to the sky as the wind swirled around me and over my fingers, carrying the scent of my blood.

The Watcher shuddered.

A single drop of my blood fell onto the snow. The Watcher stiffened, reared back. It growled softly, almost puzzled-sounding. I raised my head and looked it in the face.

"I am a Weaver," I whispered to him. "My ancestors made you. Did you know that, Watcher?"

The beast was silent.

I raised my hand. The blood was seeping down my fingers. The Watcher hissed, took a step back, and turned for the forest. With a final twitch of its tail, it vanished into the shadows.

I stepped back and looked around. The second Watcher had also vanished. Jonn and Everiss were gone along with the second horse, and the hoof prints in the snow led toward Echlos.

Atticus lay fallen, his neck at a wrong angle. I gazed at him, numb, before I stooped to pick up the gun he'd dropped. My father's gun. He'd almost killed me with my father's gun.

I slid it into my belt and wiped the blood on my finger in the snow. I bent to take Atticus's pulse.

He was dead.

I crossed to Jacob and found him dead also. I bent and closed his eyes, my heart aching at the loss of him. He'd been a good man. He'd saved my life.

"Thank you," I whispered to him.

I crossed the frozen field alone toward Echlos. I'd need help from the others to move the bodies and give them a proper burial.

My mind spiraled with what lay ahead. We would have to find permanent shelter for the fugitives and contact the Thorns. The agents were scattered, captured, dead. I was in no position to lead the operations here. And my friends...my heart twisted when I thought of Ann, Adam. I clenched my hands into fists. We would get them back, somehow. I would figure out a way.

Because I was a Weaver.

Don't miss book 4 in The Frost Chronicles—
***Bluewing*—coming Spring 2013!**

Be sure to sign up for my new releases newsletter (http://thesouthernscrawl.blogspot.com/p/new-

releases-newsletter.html) to be notified as soon as it releases!

ACKNOWLEDGEMENTS

Scott—you are my strongest supporter, my first reader for every manuscript, my perfect life partner, and my beloved friend and husband. Thank you for all the work you've poured into this project. You make every book better with your insightful comments, ideas, and suggestions. Without your encouragement and support I would never have gotten this far. Heck, I probably never would have gotten anywhere at all. I love you so much. Thank you for being my "Barnabas!"

My family—thank you for all your enthusiasm for this series and for every book I write. Your kind words encourage me and your bragging embarrasses (and secretly pleases) me. Thanks for telling your friends and coworkers about my books. Thanks for proofreading manuscripts. Thanks for your unflagging support for me and my writing. I love you all. (And no, Dad, Cole was not secretly a good guy after all.)

Mom—thank you for reading over my manuscripts again and again and giving tireless feedback. You are awesome.

Charles—your motivational strategies and enthusiastic encouragement helped me write the latter half of this book. Seriously, I don't know what I would have done without them. Thank you for brainstorming plot ideas, keeping me on track with all those work threads and chats, and for teaching me the power of the word *friend*. You're the best.

Mellie—thank you for cheering me on, letting me hijack your work threads with my own vocational woes, and talking me up to librarians. Thank you for being so enthusiastic about finding ways to promote me. You are a darling.

Every friend who has been a cheerleader on G+ when I moan about writing—Daniel D, Dru D, Wendy P, Charles W, Mellie W, Sarah D, and everyone else—thank you all. I am a communal creature and I need the support. You guys are fantastic.

Dani Crabtree—thank you for being such an amazing editor. Collaborating with you has been a dream, as always. Your comments are insightful and your generosity of spirit toward independents is massively appreciated. You're a gem!

All my awesome readers—thank you to everyone who has emailed, messaged, or tweeted me about my books. Your love for my characters and stories keeps me going. I write for you guys. These stories are my gift to you. Without you, they are just words on a page. Your imaginations bring them to life. So thank you for reading them.

ABOUT THE AUTHOR

Kate Avery Ellison lives in Atlanta, Georgia, with her husband and two spoiled (but extremely lovable) cats. She loves dark chocolate, fairy tale retellings, and love stories with witty banter and sizzling, unspoken feelings.

When she isn't working on her next writing project, Kate can most often be found reading, watching one of her favorite TV shows, working on an endless list of DIY household projects, or hanging out with friends.

You can find more information about Kate Avery Ellison's books and other upcoming projects online at http://thesouthernscrawl.blogspot.com/.

Made in the USA
Charleston, SC
23 July 2014